Total-E-Bound Publishing books by Bailey Bradford:

Southwestern Shifters

Rescued
Relentless
Reckless
Rendered
Resilience
Reverence
Revolution
Revenge

I0546045

Southern Spirits

A Subtle Breeze
When the Dead Speak
All of the Voices
Wait Until Dawn
Aftermath
What Remains
Ascension

Love in Xxchange

Rory's Last Chance
Miles to Go
Bend
What Matters Most
Ex's and O's
A Bit of Me
A Bit of You
In My Arms Tonight
Where There's A Will

Leopard's Spots

Levi
Oscar
Timothy
Isaiah
Gilbert
Esau
Sullivan
Wesley

Mossy Glenn Ranch
Chaps and Hope
Ropes and Dreams

Yes, Forever
Yes, Forever: Part One
Yes, Forever: Part Two
Yes, Forever: Part Three
Yes, Forever: Part Four
Yes, Forever: Part Five

BREAKING THE DEVIL

BAILEY BRADFORD

Breaking the Devil
ISBN # 978-1-78184-618-6
©Copyright Bailey Bradford 2013
Cover Art by Posh Gosh ©Copyright April 2013
Interior text design by Claire Siemaszkiewicz
Total-E-Bound Publishing

Published in 2013 by Total-E-Bound Publishing, Think Tank, Ruston Way, Lincoln, LN6 7FL, United Kingdom.

Total-E-Bound Publishing is an imprint of Total-E-Ntwined Limited.

BREAKING THE DEVIL

Dedication

You know it's for you.

Chapter One

Sometimes Mack wondered what the hell he'd been thinking, to spend his life in Texas when he could have moved on once his father passed away. Maybe before then, even, but it'd have been one hell of a fight.

His father had been a controlling man, claiming his family more as property than as loved ones. Even from the grave, he'd probably have found a way to drag Mack home if he'd ever tried to leave.

Lord, he was getting fanciful. *Too many years in the heat, probably cooked something upstairs.*

Summers in Texas were brutal, cooking a man from the inside out, it seemed. August in particular was a real bitch, with temperatures frequently hitting triple digits.

He should have moved somewhere like Montana, although he'd probably have died from shock when the temperature dipped below freezing. Still, he'd have got out of Texas, seen a little more of the US of A than just his part of the Lonestar State.

Oh well, what's done is done. I got my life here, and if I don't like it, ain't no one to blame but myself.

"Hey, boss, I'm gonna go check the fence along the west pasture, make sure Rancy patched it up right."

Mack grunted at Fred, one of the newer hands he'd hired — newer being relative as Fred had been there for about two years now. He waved Fred off and was left alone again with his thoughts, which was never a good thing. Mack snorted at his melancholy mood and strode from his porch across the dusty yard.

He knew where he wanted to go — the same place he kept finding himself drawn to again and again here lately. There wasn't a reason for him not to. He had a few minutes, and the hands were all out working. He could indulge himself in a few minutes of observation.

Mack stopped at the corral under the hot Texas sun, sweat trickling down his back to pool at the waistband of his jeans from the short walk he'd taken. Another few hours and he'd be soaked and smelling as rank as one of his bulls.

Well, he wasn't the only one, and a hard day's work should leave a man sweaty and in need of a good scrubbing. Preferably with someone else doing the scrubbing for him, but that wasn't going to happen. *No use thinking on what it'd be like if it did.*

Mack redirected his train of thought to something useful, like what he'd come out here to look at. He cocked his hip and propped one booted foot on the lowest wooden rail, his arms resting on the top one as he watched the beast inside the corral snort and paw at the ground.

Inside the corral stood the meanest, foulest stallion he'd ever seen — and also the most magnificent. A huge horse, too, his size matching his nasty disposition. Mack wondered half the time why he'd ever bothered buying the damn critter. The other half of the time he admitted it was because he didn't like anything that was easy, not in most cases, at least. While he didn't want a horse that was going to stomp him to death, he did like a challenge.

As the sun shone onto the horse's coat, Mack couldn't help but notice how that deep, dark colour reminded him of things better left forgotten. Of one man, specifically, that he wished he could forget. He'd had rich auburn hair and a temperament not dissimilar to that of the pissed-off horse now before Mack. Years ago, that temper the red-haired man had wielded had flamed hot and burned into a passion so fierce it'd left scars behind.

Shaking his head, Mack pushed back the memories of Justin. There was no use in dragging back up all that pain and longing. He'd already wasted way too much time on what-ifs and maybes. He should have learnt his lesson many times over, but one thing he had in common with that ornery red horse—he was pretty damned stubborn too. Just not stubborn enough to keep those memories buried where they belonged.

The heat must have melted his resolve because Justin kept popping up in his thoughts. It was a waste of time, because Justin was long freakin' gone, and Mack figured that he had never meant more to the man than a fast fuck, a way to get off.

Hell, he didn't just figure it, he *knew* it. Hadn't Justin told him so himself? Yeah, he'd broken something inside Mack all those years ago.

Sometime since, Mack had heard that Justin had joined up in the military—the Marines, specifically. He was supposed to have all sorts of medals and such. Used to be every now and then when Mack was in town, he would overhear Justin's daddy talking about his son's accomplishments, but Mack's pride kept him from making any inquiries.

If he'd had enough pride, Mack figured he wouldn't have even given enough of a shit to listen to the gossip. But those talons of need Justin had dug into him long ago had never been completely disengaged.

The old man had been dead for a while now, and Mack hadn't heard anything else about Justin for a good while. Strange, really, because his tiny little hometown was a hive of gossip. *Guess there ain't no one who knows anything about Justin, so they can't talk about him.*

Well, regardless, he reckoned it was a good thing he had just been an experiment. That way Justin hadn't had to worry about that whole Don't Ask, Don't Tell thing. Mack would bet even with it being lifted, there was still plenty of problems facing anyone who wasn't straight in the military. Hell, unless you was straight, you couldn't marry in most states, and your spouse didn't get military benefits anyway even if the marriage was done up all legal.

"Enough already," he scolded himself. It was a certainty that Justin hadn't wasted years—*years*—dwelling on what might have been. Normally Mack didn't think on it so heavily himself, but that angry red horse just stirred up memories. He really shouldn't have agreed to tame the damn critter.

The stallion snorted, pawing at the ground and tossing its head, sending that silky mane rippling in the faint afternoon breeze.

"Fuckin' red devil." Mack reached slowly into his shirt pocket to pull out a few sugar cubes. He was vaguely aware of hoof beats coming from off to the side, but didn't pay any attention since he figured it was just one of the hands coming back in from working.

Mack concentrated on keeping his body relaxed, his voice low and smooth and sweet. The words didn't matter so much, but the tone... Well, that was the trick, wasn't it? Making a mean beast listen to you, lulling it into complacency — or at least out of murderous intent. Mack extended his arm, sugar cubes in hand. Bribing the beautiful bastard hadn't worked yet, but maybe eventually it would.

"Shit!" Mack jerked away from the corral as the stallion charged at him, rearing high in the air and bringing those deadly hooves down like hell's condemnation. They missed the slat by mere inches. Mack stumbled back a few steps, his heart slamming against his ribs — then promptly flailed forward when he bounced off a hard surface. A hard, living surface.

Two strong arms reached out and caught him, and Mack's breath gusted from him. He could have sworn his heart went from jackhammering to a complete stop.

Just like that, he knew from the brief touch — just from the scent that had hit him the very second his back had made contact with the broad chest — oh, he knew from the way his body flooded with lust and his cock snapped to attention...

Justin was back.

Chapter Two

Justin had had a plan, really. He was going to win Mack over with sweet talk and patience, but the moment he saw Mack, the moment he got close enough to touch the man who'd haunted him for over a decade, every good intention Justin had vanished. Lust and a possessiveness that almost crushed him as it tangled up with need and love had him locking his arms around Mack as the man stumbled back, startled by the big red stallion trying to get out of the corral.

Justin's dick went from mildly interested to damn near stone as he held Mack for a second and just absorbed everything about him. Despite the years gone by, Mack still had that sweat and leather scent that flipped every one of Justin's switches. A sniff of the man had Justin's cock throbbing, pre-cum leaking from the tip, but he didn't dare let Mack know. How the hell had he waited so long to hold Mack again?

How had he ever let him go?

Justin had asked himself that so many times over the years.

"Hello, Mack," he said, loosening his hold on Mack even though he wanted to hold onto him forever. Justin had no illusions—Mack was furious with him. He completely understood why, too.

He just hoped to hell and high Heaven that Mack wouldn't kill him outright before he had a chance to win Mack back.

* * * *

Justin's voice was like a dagger to the heart and a stroke of a tongue to Mack's cock at the same time. It was a disconcerting experience, and Mack could hardly even breathe as he tried to think.

Somehow, somehow, he had to turn. Mack knew he had to find the strength to face the man who had consumed so much of his life. Finally managing to take a deep breath and feed his starving lungs, Mack calmly, coolly—he hoped—pulled himself out from the hold Justin had on his shoulder still. Turning and affecting a casual look, Mack faced his own red devil. *Well, goddamn.* How he kept his legs from giving out was beyond him, and how he spoke, that had to be a miracle, he figured.

"Hello, Justin." Mack tried not to be too obvious about the hunger coursing through him as he swept Justin with his gaze. It probably didn't show, not with all the anger and pain that was bubbling up and trying to spew out of him. Mack tried to absorb the changes in the man without staring. He would have thought Justin had been conjured here, since he'd just been reminiscing about him.

Except, if that were the case, if Mack had the power to make the man he longed for just *poof* appear, Justin would have been there years ago—like twelve years ago.

Mack pressed a hand to his belly, some dull ache there drawing his attention just a bit. God, it was like being kicked in the stomach, seeing Justin again. The man stood there with some kind of smirk in place, letting Mack look him over. Mack had no doubt Justin was getting his jollies out of knowing what a damned stud he was.

If Mack had been able to, he'd have turned away then and walked off. But he couldn't, not yet. For all he knew, it'd be another dozen years before he saw Justin again. *If* he ever saw him again.

Even though Mack wanted to let his gaze linger, to memorise every detail, there was no way he could. Or at least, no way he'd let himself do it any longer than he already had. He didn't want Justin to see the desperation that was almost overwhelming all the resentment and hate Mack had carried towards the man for so long. And that, he knew, would be dangerous to what was left of his heart and soul.

The problem was, Justin wasn't making it easy for Mack to stop ogling him. He used his eyes like hands, burning trails over Mack's skin. Mack started to take a step back when Justin levelled his gaze with his, but Mack caught himself before he actually moved.

He wasn't afraid of Justin, at least not physically. Ah, but God, his heart couldn't survive another round with him. Mack wasn't sure his mind had survived the last round intact, either. After all, what sane person would still be hanging on to something that had happened so long ago?

Right then Justin's lips hitched up on one side, making Mack suspect that Justin was aware of his impulse to step back. That half-smile should have probably been a warning for Mack—he'd seen it often enough when they'd been dumb kids and Justin had come up with some plan that was likely to get their hides skinned if they got caught.

But Mack's brain was still trying to figure out what the hell was going on. That was the only reason he could come up with as to why he didn't jump back or resist when Justin reached out for him, those big hands of his curling around Mack's shoulders.

He was jerked forward so hard that he let out a grunt when his body slammed against Justin's. *Sweet God have mercy*—Mack's thought shattered then because Justin's mouth was on his, claiming it with lips, tongue and teeth.

Claiming him.

No. I ain't his. Mack didn't end the kiss, though. Instead he grabbed a hold of Justin's shirt in both hands and kissed Justin back with the same fierce need, sucking Justin's tongue like he wanted to suck his cock. That realisation was like being dunked in ice water, and Mack jerked away, letting go of Justin even as he freed himself from the man's grip.

Mack took a few steps back and tried to get himself under control. His body was all for jumping Justin immediately, just fucking him in the middle of the yard, screw whoever might see them. He glanced at Justin and found some relief in knowing that the man was struggling to get his breath under control. At least Mack wasn't the only one affected so strongly there.

Once he was pretty sure he could keep his shit together, Mack looked at Justin. He would be calm, cool, collected—all that crap which meant he'd be the epitome of control.

"What the fuck, man?" burst from his lips. Well, maybe he'd be that other controlled man later, because right now all he wanted to do was hit something. More specifically, someone.

Chapter Three

Justin didn't snarl back even though Mack's temper fuelled his own. Mack had every right to be pissed off, and Justin didn't—but that didn't mean Justin was going to turn heel and leave.

It was probably one of the hardest things he'd ever done, but Justin held himself still, except for the smile he slowly let slide into place. That smile had let him get away with more than he should have on many an occasion, and he was hoping now wouldn't prove an exception.

He could see the stark outline of Mack's cock through his jeans. A wet spot spread slowly on the faded material. Justin's own dick was fair to dribbling like a faucet with a worn-out washer. He curled his hands into fists to keep from grabbing at Mack again. It'd be pure perfection to bend that cowboy over the nearest surface and fuck him into oblivion. Mack had filled out, the boy he had been still evident under the thicker form of the man he'd become. Broader shoulders, harsher features, time and the sun having carved Mack into every man's fantasy cowboy.

And Mack was looking at him with a hunger that Justin wasn't going to be able to resist. He might not be able to fuck Mack right then like he wanted, but he could sure give them both something to think about. Something to tide them both over until they got inside — if Mack would let him inside. Justin was sure Mack was up for a little relief.

The way Mack was eyein' his groin, Justin halfway expected Mack to wrestle him to the ground then and there. The idea of that happening, of Mack shoving him down and ripping at his clothes, of him fucking Justin until Justin couldn't even scream — that was a wicked, hot fantasy that had Justin clenching his ass, that little hidden spot between his cheeks feeling warm and needy.

No one had ever affected him like Mack. All the years he'd been in the Marines, hiding who he truly was, Justin had never bothered getting close to anyone. Even after the repeal of Don't Ask, Don't Tell, he'd kept people at a distance. It'd been ingrained in him by then, the need for secrecy. Justin had thought that would never change, but now, seeing Mack, every restraint he'd ever put in place snapped in two. He knew if Mack kept watching him like that, he'd be unable to stop himself from touching Mack again.

Justin looked him over, head to toe. Mack's cowboy hat had gone flying at some point, he didn't know when. He didn't particularly care either. Mack's nipples ached, his cock ached, his damn balls were already pulled up and ready to send cum pumping up his rod.

Justin narrowed his eyes and Mack felt his nipples pucker and grow hard, the material of his shirt suddenly rougher than sandpaper against them. Justin smiled in a way that made Mack almost cream his jeans. It was the sexiest smile he'd ever seen, and his cock pulsed and swelled, eager to be touched.

Somehow, Justin knew it, too. Mack didn't know how, but there was a confidence in the way Justin held himself that hadn't been there when Justin had been a boy still. And that was the last time Mack had seen him, so he honestly couldn't say he knew Justin now, could he?

Even so, when Justin lowered his eyes slowly, so fucking slowly, down to Mack's dick, Justin's smile seemed to stretch and get even hotter. Goddamn, Mack could feel the heat of that gaze like an actual touch, but he bit back the whimper that would have let Justin know it. Giving Justin any such clue would be handing over power to the one person Mack wouldn't ever trust again.

Mack thought Justin was going to ignore his unanswered question, and his temper flared hotter as he repeated it. "I said, what the fuck?"

Justin finally raised his eyes back up to Mack's and the heat in them almost had his knees buckling. "Not 'what', nuh-uh, cowboy," Justin purred, moving right back into him until he'd brought their bodies flush up against each other. Mack couldn't have moved back if his life had depended on it—and in a way, he knew it did. Justin could break him like no one else could.

Still, he stood there as Justin slid his hands around his waist. A tug and he pulled Mack's hips to his. Then Justin lowered his hands, eyes locked to Mack's. Mack's breath stuttered as he realised what Justin was doing, where those big strong hands were going.

At least all the guys are out riding fence. That was one worry gone, but Mack had a much more pressing concern. He couldn't make himself stop Justin, not at all. Justin cupped his ass with both hands and Mack wanted to melt right into the touch. Shards of desire — sharp, painful, pleasurable — shot from his ass to his dick and through his body. Holy shit, he was in serious trouble. Justin was irresistible and Mack badly needed to resist him.

"It's 'who', Mack. Who the fuck." Justin punctuated the words with a grind of his hips. Mack's eyes crossed before he shut them as he scrabbled to find a place to put his hands. He didn't want to encourage Justin.

Yes I do, fuckin' liar. I want him, I fuckin' want him so bad, more'n I want my pride.

He settled for holding onto Justin's biceps, the heavy muscles there hot and hard beneath his palms.

"I'm the 'who', Mack," Justin continued huskily. "I'm the 'who', and when I'm fucking you, you'll know it, because it'll be my name on your lips." Justin nibbled on his lips, emphasising his point. Mack kept them stubbornly sealed shut. "My name you're gonna be screaming when you come. My name you chant like a prayer…"

Hell's bells, Mack wanted to punch Justin and bend over for him both. His hands seemed to have a mind of their own, sliding down until he was palming the firm mounds of Justin's ass. Mack opened his eyes and prayed to God for some sense. Anger boiled up and he released Justin's ass like that fine flesh was scalding his hands. Instead he grabbed Justin's shirt collar and pulled his head down with it so that they were nose to nose.

"You fucked me years ago, and frankly it wasn't worth the hell you put me through. Get off my ranch." Mack shoved Justin hard, releasing his collar as he did so, but that red-haired man had always been built like a friggin' brick wall, and the years had only made him even burlier than he'd been as a kid. Mack's shove only had him taking a slight half-step backwards.

Justin's bulk might not have changed significantly, but something else had. When Mack had known Justin before, something like a shove would have had Justin going from fucking to fighting in a split second, but now his smile bloomed full force, transforming his face from merely attractive to out-and-out handsome. There were little feathery lines at the edges of his large brown eyes that hadn't been there the last time Mack had seen him, and the overall effect of his maturity was devastating to Mack's heart, not to mention his self-control or his cock.

"Maybe it wasn't worth it to you then, but I promise..." Justin paused, his seductive voice having made Mack a sufficiently stupid man at that point. He stood gaping as Justin touched his shoulders, then slid his hands down over his nipples. "I promise I will make it more than worth your while this time."

Mack mentally called himself twelve kinds of fool for not stopping Justin, not speaking up, but he couldn't get a word past the tight ball of need in his throat. That need was tied up with a lump of fear, too, because he couldn't make his feet move or his body pull away from Justin.

Goddamn it, he didn't want to pull away from Justin.

Mack's nipples hardened as Justin plucked at them and Justin inhaled sharply. "Beautiful, baby. Wish I could strip you down right out here and see..." He dragged those hands down, across Mack's abs, making them tense as Mack fought back the urge to beg for Justin to do it, just strip him down and fuck him.

Justin glanced down then back at him, and Mack was held there by those beautiful brown eyes that he feared could see right into his soul.

"Just let me touch you."

Mack had to be imagining the plea he'd heard in Justin's voice. Justin wouldn't ever beg him for anything. Yet Mack didn't protest as Justin slanted his mouth over his, then Mack was being devoured again, his cock stroked through his jeans as Justin thrust his tongue repeatedly against Mack's.

Mack's cock leaked copiously as Justin's touch became more demanding, milking him through his jeans. His knees trembled and his balls drew even tighter. *Oh shit, oh shit! I can't stop, don't even wanna stop. Don't ever wanna stop.*

Mack was vaguely aware of Justin popping the button open on Mack's jeans, then the metallic sound of the zipper sliding down reached his ears. Mack's spine tingled as anticipation stole his breath, and finally, finally, Justin shoved his hand inside Mack's underwear to grasp his cock.

"Mmph." Mack might have meant 'please' or 'more' or 'wait', he wasn't sure. Not until he had a flash image of Justin backing off—then he knew which one of those he definitely hadn't meant.

Justin encircled the head of Mack's cock. He ran his thumb over the slit of it before pressing firmly. Mack shook all the way down to his toes, want curling in his gut, stark and sharp. Justin smeared the pre-cum leaking out over Mack's tip while shoving at Mack's jeans and drawers with his other hand.

As soon as Mack felt Justin holding his balls and at the same time fisting his cock, something damn near short-circuited in his head. He whimpered as he exhaled then promptly bit his lips since Justin wasn't kissing him anymore.

Mack slid his hands up and held onto Justin's broad shoulders as Justin began stroking him, his hands rough and hot and perfect. Justin kissed him again then, this one more teeth than tongue, more dominance than tenderness as Justin took even more control. Mack's lips were bitten and sucked, his tongue wrestled into submission as Justin owned him in that moment.

Except he knew Justin had always owned him.

No, no, he hasn't, he can't… But goddamn, what he does to me —

"Come for me, cowboy," Justin grated out, thrusting against Mack even as he sped up the strokes to Mack's dick. "Let me see you, smell you. Fuck, I want your hand on me too, or your mouth, so pretty…" Justin dipped his head again and nipped Mack's bottom lip, and Mack shivered hard enough to rattle his bones.

"Want your ass riding my cock, gotta see you coming apart for me." It sounded almost like Justin was begging, even though the words were hot and wicked. Mack couldn't make sense of it, then Justin twisted his hand around, rubbing Mack's cockhead but good, and Mack hissed as pleasure surged from his balls and right on out of his dick. Hot, thick ropes of cum shot out over Justin's hands, some splattering his arms and shirt. Mack just managed to keep his eyes open to watch, entranced by the way his spunk looked pouring out onto Justin.

"Look what you do to me," Justin growled, pulling Mack's hand to his own denim-encased cock. He thrust and Mack curled his hand around as much of the large shaft as he could. His orgasm had left him stupid, that was why he didn't jerk his hand back, was why he moved closer and rubbed eagerly against Justin's dick.

Justin's breath came in harsh pants as he pistoned his hips harder and harder, driving his length against Mack's hand. Mack pressed with more of his body, leaning towards Justin, letting him rut all over him. His pride wasn't quite demolished. Mack kept himself from begging Justin to come, just barely.

Instead he nudged his other hand between Justin's legs, giving him some pressure to his nuts, and Justin yelled as he went still. He jerked Mack up against him until Mack was as close as he could possibly get with his hands between them.

Mack would have sworn his knees had turned to gelatin and he wondered if he was going to be able to stay upright with the way Justin was grinding and groaning against him. Then Justin was right there, his climax spilling warm through the denim of his jeans. Mack wished that wet seed was pouring right into his palm so he could hold Justin's essence in his hand. Damn it, he was getting silly, fanciful thoughts, probably just because he'd finally got off with someone else instead of all alone.

"Shit, you burn me alive, love," Justin murmured.

Mack jerked back, because one thing he knew for certain despite his ridiculous musings was that Justin didn't love him. You didn't leave someone, break their heart and shred their soul, not if you loved 'em. "I don't think so," Mack snarled as he fought to get away from Justin without appearing as panicked as he suddenly felt. "I surely don't, no, sir."

He reined in and pushed aside that kernel of hope trying to bloom upon hearing Justin's slip of the tongue. Twelve years of nothing, not a single goddamned word, not a letter, not even a cheesy-ass postcard. He used that thought to beat away anything but the anger and the hurt.

"You got your rocks off. Ain't it time for you to leave again?" Mack asked, keeping his voice low and cold as he righted his clothing. For a second he thought he saw a flash of pain in Justin's expression, but he dismissed it. He didn't have any kind of power over Justin, certainly not the kind to hurt the man. "Wouldn't want you to vary off track. You oughta disappear for another twelve years after this, so get gone." Mack wouldn't be able to resist him if he intended to stay anywhere nearby.

"Now get on and get off my ranch," he said as he gestured dismissively. "You got whatever the hell you wanted, and I got work to do."

Justin glared, but Mack wasn't the least bit intimidated. He'd grown plenty, too, and he was capable of kicking Justin's ass...maybe. "I mean it, bub. Get the fuck off my property." Although, Justin had been in the Marines for a long time, so he could probably break Mack into a hundred pieces with a flick of his fingers. So why was he still bitching at Justin? *Because I know he won't hurt me, not physically at least. Doesn't mean I trust him in any way. I won't let it mean that.*

Justin narrowed his eyes and the corner of his mouth turned up in a smug grin. "Oh, you got your rocks off just as surely as I did, cowboy. You came so hard I thought you was gonna pass out." Justin glanced down Mack's body and that grin amped up in smugness. "Looks like you're ready to go again, too. I'd be more than happy to help you out. Again."

Mack's cheekbones flared with heat that raced down to his neck and chest. It wasn't all embarrassment, either, because Justin's astounding arrogance turned

Mack on. He didn't care for that fact at all. If he wasn't real careful, he'd be dropping to his hands and knees and begging Justin to fuck him. Mack would rather let that evil red horse stomp his skull in.

"Doesn't mean you're the one to take care of it, now does it?" Mack pointed out rather snarkily. He was surprised he hadn't spat the words out with enough venom to kill the man. He'd beat off a hundred times before he let Justin touch him again. Before he let Justin know just how badly he wanted to feel his mouth sucking him dry.

Aw, shit! Now there's a visual I don't need at this particular moment. Later, when I'm alone, maybe, but not now with that temptin' fucker standing there looking like the answer to every prayer I ever had.

Justin took a step forward, and there, in his eyes, Mack saw that red devil's temper that the man had kept banked so far. Damned if seeing it didn't make his cock twitch with lust. Justin brought a hand up to Mack's jaw, and Mack found himself unable to pull away as that rough hand cupped his face. Justin rubbed his thumb over Mack's bottom lip and molten lust coiled in Mack's groin.

"Let me clear something up for you," Justin said as he kept tracing Mack's lip. His voice had a low, mean timbre to it that wasn't doing a damn thing to quell Mack's desire. In fact, it sent goose bumps fuelled by anticipation racing all over Mack's body. "You already agreed to break the horses for JMR Ranch, starting with that stallion there in the corral."

Mack knew his eyes had to be huge, and he halfway expected them to pop right out of his fool head as his stomach lurched. Surely he hadn't heard that right, surely his hormones had overpowered his hearing or something—but Justin looked so damned full of himself, those brown eyes of his sparkling as he smirked.

"Yeah, I see you're beginning to get the picture now. The JMR is my ranch, cowboy, and unless you decide not to honour your word..." Justin paused, arching one auburn eyebrow at him.

"I always keep my word," Mack snapped, sounding too shrill but unable to tone it down. He was cornered, damn it, and he hated that. Hated feeling helpless and trapped. He'd known the neighbouring ranch had been sold, but Mack had never been particularly chatty and so hadn't paid any attention to the gossip over who'd bought it. Now he really, really wished he had. "But you should know, I'd never have agreed to take on the JMR's horses if I'd even suspected that you owned the damn ranch." The anger he felt at the manipulation slapped the nerves right out of his voice. "If you hadn't tricked me, sent over your foreman with an offer instead of coming yourself—" Mack glared so hard his head ached from it. He didn't bother to tone down the disgust he was feeling then. "If you had been an *honest* man, that red stallion wouldn't be in my corral, and you sure as shit wouldn't be standing here. I'd have made sure you knew you weren't welcome."

Mack stepped back, uncaring now if it appeared cowardly. He needed out of Justin's reach, needed the man to quit touching him. "But you weren't honest. You lied, tricked me, whatever, however, just so long's you got what you wanted, right, bub?" Mack shrugged and went on before Justin could answer, because whatever Justin had to say just didn't matter. "Well, no big deal, huh? 'Cause even though you're a lyin' son of a bitch, I ain't, and I'll do what I said I would do."

The insulting words seemed to roll right off Justin, who merely watched him with a hunger that didn't dim. "That's what I'm counting on, cowboy. You always keep your word, don't you? No matter how long ago you gave it?"

Justin tensed then, Mack could see it in the way he held his shoulders and in the corded tendons of his neck. He watched Mack like a hawk, and Mack suddenly knew why. His stomach dipped like he was on the big-drop of a rollercoaster, and that hope he'd tried to beat to death pushed right up into his heart. He stared at Justin, fearing very much that his soul was laid bare to the man. He prayed it wasn't so. He had to have some way to save himself.

"Yes or no?" Justin asked, the lines around the outer edges of his eyes becoming more pronounced. Something that seemed to be an awful lot like his pride dried up deep inside Mack.

"Yes, Justin, always," Mack scraped out, closing his eyes as shame washed over him. How could Justin still affect him after all this time? Panic was riding him hard, because Mack knew damn good and well what Justin was referring to, and it wasn't breaking horses.

No, he was talking about something else altogether, something that Mack had fervently hoped Justin would have forgotten. He didn't know why Justin hadn't forgotten it, since he'd never meant shit to Justin. He sent up a silent prayer that he would make it through the door as he opened his eyes and tried to rush past Justin.

God apparently wasn't interested in Mack's issues at that time, however, because Justin grabbed his arm and stopped him in his tracks. Justin didn't speak, didn't let go of Mack, either. Nope, that stubborn man waited until Mack had to look at him or punch him, and the only reason Mack did the former was because the latter would end up with Justin far too close to him again.

So Mack looked at him, and Justin smiled in a way that had Mack's heart fluttering, which was bad, and his dick hardening, which was also bad no matter how good it felt.

"That vow, Mack, the one you made me before I left—that's what says I *am* the one to 'take care of it' for you." Justin gripped him tighter, almost painfully so, showing in that hold the anger he had been suppressing.

Mack glanced at Justin's hand where it was curled around his upper arm, then back at Justin. He couldn't think. Everything was swirling around in his head like a huge tornado had been let loose in there. Memories and love—and always, always the pain. The feelings blended together, spinning like some hellish carousel straight out of the scariest horror novel. Mack shook his head, hoping to knock some coherent thoughts into line, and he tugged his arm out of Justin's grasp.

All these years, he had thought of a million things he would say to Justin if he ever saw him again, but now every single one of those things abandoned him. Giving up any hope of expressing years' worth of anger and pain, he turned his back on Justin and bolted. His pride would just have to recover from him fleeing, because Mack couldn't stay near Justin another second without doing something he'd regret.

Mack ran up the steps and thundered over the porch. He jerked the screen door open and went inside without looking back. Doing so would lead to him running right back to Justin and begging for things Mack knew they could never have. He shut the door, then shut the wooden door as well.

He'd not be finding a moment's peace to work with the horses, and trying to tame anything when he was riled up and a jittery mess would end up with either him or the horse getting hurt. It was a damn good thing he'd sent all the hands out. It wouldn't have done for them to see him like that, all moon-eyed and stupid over a guy who'd trounced his heart. Mack didn't want anyone to think of him as weak, but inside…inside he knew.

Justin was his kryptonite, his Delilah, his weakness, and even without them having sex, Mack knew he was fucked six ways to Sunday.

Somehow he'd made it into his bathroom. Mack didn't remember walking in there, but he stood now with his arms braced on the sink as he sucked in several deep breaths. When he could, he finally raised his head up and checked himself in the mirror, studying the face staring back at him. Blue eyes, dark hair, sun-browned skin—there wasn't anything special about him. Cowboys were a dime a dozen in this part of Texas, and he'd bet there were even some other gay ones around if that was still Justin's thing.

Although, judging by Mack's swollen red lips and the cum staining his pants, what was Justin's thing wasn't even in doubt. Justin had wanted him, had really touched him and would have done more if Mack had let him. Mack wanted to, so badly, but Jesus, his chest hurt with memories and pain.

It showed in his expression gawking back at him, that devastation he was feeling. His eyes blurred and he blinked before the tears could fall. He'd wasted enough on Justin already—enough tears, enough time, enough hope. Enough anger.

Mack turned away and started stripping out of his clothes. He finished that then started the shower, turning on the cold only because he needed the jolt of it. He stepped under the icy blast, and despite his best attempts at restraint, tears began to fall.

"I can't do this, I just can't," Mack murmured to himself, to God, to anyone and nothing. He was already aching so much inside that he was afraid he would shatter. He scrubbed at his face and tried to wash away the tears along with the feel of Justin from his lips. It was no use, though, and Mack cursed as he realised that Justin's taste was inside him like some bitter seed he'd swallowed. It'd sprouted up already and taken root, threatening to fill him with everything he could remember about Justin.

Mad at himself, at Justin, at the whole universe, even, Mack slapped the water off and shoved the shower door open. He grabbed a towel and rubbed his hair with quick, rough strokes before wrapping the towel around his waist. He didn't have time to be this miserable, whining shit he was becoming. Mack would be damned if he let Justin have this kind of power over him again.

Damned.

Chapter Four

All the self-control Justin had developed courtesy of the United States Marine Corps hadn't been enough to keep him from mauling Mack. Justin couldn't even make himself regret it, because he'd lived with the need for the other man for half his life or longer. He couldn't have been more than fourteen or fifteen when he'd begun to realise that he loved Mack Williams. They'd been friends for so long at that point, Justin had at first believed he was confusing a kind of fraternal love with another more forbidden type.

The things he'd started fantasising about doing to Mack surely weren't ones the people in their ranching community would tolerate. Justin had feared for his life as a kid, just because of the thoughts he'd had.

As a man, he was willing to risk whatever he had to in order to have Mack again. Justin had been a fool once before, had let fear win, and it'd cost him a dozen years that he could have been spending with Mack. Now he was going to have to pray to God that Mack would forgive him.

Justin had seen the need in Mack's eyes, felt it in the hardness of his cock, the wet puffs of his breath as he'd come. He'd heard it in those shaky, soft noises as Mack had given Justin his release. Jesus, Mack had felt perfect, all hot and hard and smooth skin over steely dick.

Justin closed his eyes for a moment as Minx walked, the quarter horse knowing the way back to the ranch. He and Minx had made this trip often enough over the past couple of weeks. Maybe it made him into some kind of stalker, but Justin hadn't been able to stay away from Mack. He'd watched for as long as he had been able to, and the first chance he'd had of getting the man alone, Justin had reined the mare right on into Mack's yard.

Mack had been so busy eyeing that bitch of a red horse that he hadn't even heard Justin's approach. Justin's mind reeled as he replayed seeing Mack up close for that first time again, feeling his muscled body, the scent and flavour of the man...

It made him have to shift in the saddle, his cock erect and aching as he opened his eyes. If he kept them closed much longer, he'd end up having to beat off before he made it back to his place. Mack just did it for him in a way no one else ever had.

"Come on, Minx, let's move," he urged as he lightly nudged the mare with his heels. She was a smart girl, didn't take to force at all, but a little encouragement and a soft touch would have Minx following your every command.

Minx's black coat gleamed under the bright sun, a slight sheen of sweat forming a foam in spots by the time they reached his house. "Good girl," he murmured as he dismounted. "It's too hot for you to be ridden any more today. By four it'll be well over a hundred, and that'd bake your pretty hide."

Justin kept on talking to Minx as he removed the saddle and blanket. He set them aside—he'd put them up later. Right now he wanted to give Minx a treat. Justin cupped the horse under the muzzle and rubbed. "Bet you'd like to be rinsed off, wouldn't you?"

Talking to the horse didn't make him crazy. Justin had seen the way a voice could soothe an animal, just like it could soothe another human being. Mack's voice could sure as hell stimulate him in ways that were going to be keeping Justin awake tonight.

He wanted to get inside and clean himself off, but then again, he didn't. It might have been silly, but he could smell Mack on him and wasn't in a hurry to lose that scent.

Then again, he didn't intend to be without it for long. Justin was determined to win Mack over. He wouldn't be put off by Mack's anger or harsh words, because Mack wanted him, needed him even, Justin would bet. It would be pride that stood in their way, his and Mack's both. Justin might well have to beg— really, truly, drop to his knees and beg. It might ruin something in him, but if it got him Mack's forgiveness, if it earned him Mack's love again, then Justin would give up anything he had for that.

After adjusting his cock so that it wasn't rubbing so uncomfortably against the seam of his jeans, Justin walked over to the spigot and turned on the water. "I'm coming," he told Minx as he picked up the hose. The horse neighed as he began wetting her down.

Some people might gripe about the way a wet horse smelt, just like some did wet dogs, but Justin had always enjoyed the odour. Or maybe it was the whole experience, running his hands over such beautiful horse flesh, knowing all that strength was right under his fingers.

Minx played it up, too, shaking her mane out and splattering water all over. Justin laughed and made sure she'd had a good rinse before putting her out to pasture. Minx took off for the shade, snorting and pounding the ground in a display of what Justin took as horse-happiness.

"Looks like you could use a rinse down yourself," a familiar voice called out.

Justin turned from watching Minx to find his foreman Craig standing a few yards behind him, cowboy hat pulled low over his eyes to shield them from the sun.

"Yup, that's next on my list." Justin took his own hat off and casually held it in front of his groin. "Anything I need to know about right now?"

Craig shrugged and tucked his thumbs in the front of his jeans pockets. "Nope, don't think so. Benny and Jeremy are still out in the west pasture getting the cattle settled in, but they ought to be back soon. You gonna feed us or do I gotta cook dinner?"

"I'll do it," Justin huffed, rolling the brim of his hat against his palm. "Won't be anything fancy, 'cause you know cooking wasn't my job in the Marines, but it won't kill us. Need to hire on a cook when we can." Once the ranch got going, or when he won Mack over. Right now Justin had to be careful over how much he spent hiring out help. He was damned glad Craig had been willing to come work for him once they'd both finished up their last tour of duty.

Craig nodded and took his own hat off, swiping at his brow. "It's hotter'n hell today. How'd the visit with the neighbour go? He seemed like an all right guy when I met him to get him contracted with us."

Justin glanced down, the sun suddenly even hotter where it hit the back of his neck. How much should he share with Craig? They'd never discussed their personal lives much when they'd served together, but Justin had kind of thought Craig was like him since he'd never known of the guy having a date.

Sighing, Justin figured he was just going to have to risk it. If Craig quit on him, he was fucked, but it was better to have him pack up and leave now than later on, probably.

Justin quit staring at his hat and glanced up again. "Come on in for a drink while I fix dinner, and we'll talk. I gotta shower first though." He headed inside, feeling weird as hell because he didn't know how to conduct the conversation he and Craig were going to have to have.

"Just hop a squat at the table, get yourself some tea if you want it," he added over his shoulder when he heard Craig following him. "I'll be out of the shower in ten."

In the bathroom, Justin stripped quickly, grimacing when he had to unstick his pubes from his drawers. "Shoulda squirted myself off after all," he grumbled. A lukewarm shower proved too hot with the heat of the day still on his skin, so Justin turned the knob to a cooler setting and soaped himself up.

Nerves made him careless and he cursed when the shampoo got in his eyes, making them burn like a mother. Now he'd look like a major pothead when he sat down to talk to Craig.

But even that nervousness couldn't wipe out the memory of Mack, the anger and passion blazing in his blue eyes. There were so many things Justin wanted to do to Mack, so much they'd never got to try. He'd left when they had both been just eighteen, still boys growing into their bodies.

What would Mack look like now, naked and hard, lust bringing a flush over his skin? He'd be lighter on his chest and ass, even his legs and upper arms, Justin would bet. A farmer's tan was part of the cowboy outfit down here in Texas. Justin would bet that paler skin would bruise up real pretty with love bites, blues and purples and pinks, all left there by his mouth as he sucked.

Would Mack let him do that, let him mark him up? Justin groaned softly and fisted his cock. It was hard and his nuts were pulled up tight already just from thinking about Mack. He hadn't been so horny since he'd left, so he knew it was all Mack. Only Mack.

Justin braced himself against the shower wall with one hand and quickly jacked himself off with the other. It wasn't the best orgasm of his life, but he came in minutes with the vision of Mack in his head. Justin bit his lips to keep from making a sound as he thrust, gripping his cock tighter and tighter. He pumped out his load then rested his head on the wet tiles for a moment, feeling empty and lonely. It wasn't his hand he needed. It was Mack.

By the time he made it to the kitchen, a little more than ten minutes had passed. Craig was sitting with his legs out and crossed at the ankles, his head tipped back and his eyes closed. His thick arms were folded over his chest, but Justin knew Craig wasn't asleep. Craig had instincts that trounced Justin's, having been a Green Beret for more years than Justin could have ever hacked being one.

"Feel better?" Craig drawled, and Justin froze by the stove, wondering if Craig had heard him beating off after all. Craig cleared that fear up almost immediately. "Wet horse always makes me itchy. Got sensitive skin."

The incongruities of butch men. Craig can kill a person in a hundred different ways before the person even knows they're being offed, but he has sensitive skin.

"That's gonna suck ass for you come rainy season," Justin pointed out as he took a skillet from the oven.

Craig grunted and sat up, or at least, he raised his head and peered at Justin through one barely-opened eye. "You telling me South Texas has a rainy season? Isn't that like saying it rains in hell?"

Justin turned the burner on and cocked a hip as he clucked his tongue at Craig. "Now, now, man, don't you know talking like that'll get you hanged in Texas?"

Craig closed his eye again and didn't seem concerned. "Whatever. It's hotter than hell here anyway. Isn't like I'm telling lies when I say so."

"Nope, you sure aren't," Justin agreed. "And we kind of have a rainy season. Usually when the rodeo rolls in to San Antonio in February. Every now and then we even have floods. It happens."

Nothing else was said while Justin got dinner started, a simple meal of spaghetti and garlic bread since he didn't have anything else easy on hand. When he had the water boiling and the sauce bubbling, he turned back to Craig, who was now watching him. It almost made Justin more nervous, except that just wasn't possible.

"So, the thing is…" He trailed off, unable to meet Craig's gaze. That pissed him off when he realised what he was doing, because he didn't have anything to be ashamed of. Justin snapped his head up, looking into Craig's eyes. "So the thing is, I'm gay, and the neighbour, he's…he's more than just a neighbour. I aim to win him back, and if you're uncomfortable with any of that, I understand." He wouldn't like it, but he'd understand — some people were just bigoted assholes, and you never knew who would be like that from appearances alone. The nicest-seeming person could turn out to be a rabid homophobe, Justin had learnt. It was creepy as fuck.

Craig didn't say anything as he stared back at Justin, then finally he just closed his eyes again. Craig's stomach rumbled loudly and he grimaced. "Whatever, Justin, I don't give a shit who you fuck. Just feed me before I pass out."

Well, he'd worried too much about that for nothing.

"And if Benny or Jeremy have a problem with you being gay, I'll see to it they know they can pack their shit and work somewhere else," Craig said when Justin turned back to stir the sauce.

"I was worried you'd freak out on me," Justin admitted.

"Nah, kinda figured," Craig replied. "My gaydar's never worked for shit, but I recognised a kindred soul after spending enough time with you."

Justin dropped the spoon on the stove and spun around. "Are you saying — ?"

"Yup," Craig cut him off. "Now that we've had this heart-to-heart talk, can we eat?"

"We should call Benny and Jeremy over, see if they're ready for dinner."

"They'll have leftovers when they get in," Craig told him. "I haven't heard their horses so they're still out working. Probably going to have to go with them next time, because it shouldn't take them so long to get their chores done."

"But they have experience, they should know how to do their jobs," Justin pointed out. "And if there was a problem, they'd radio us. Maybe they're just taking their time riding back so's not to overheat their mounts, or their selves."

"Maybe." But something in the way Craig said it seemed odd to Justin. Did Craig suspect the other two hands of messing around...together? Or just in general?

"So, what's the story with you and the cowboy next door? Trying to get in his pants?"

Justin almost laughed at that, because Craig made it sound like some little crush, a harmless fascination maybe, but Mack was so much more than that. His heart ached though, and he didn't think he was going to answer. It surprised him when the words began to spill out.

"See, me and Mack, we grew up together. We were best friends and all that through school, then one day I realised I didn't feel like a friend towards him, you know?" Justin checked and saw Craig nod. Justin took the pasta up and walked to the sink to drain it as he talked. "So I hemmed and hawed, but eventually we figured out we both felt the same way for each other. We, uh..." Well, he didn't want to go into detail. Justin put the pasta back in the pot and set it on a hot plate. "Anyway, things just didn't go like I hoped they would, and I left. Never stopped thinking about him, never stopped wanting him."

He'd have him again, too. And this time, he wouldn't be a young, scared kid who gave up on the one thing, one person, he loved. If Mack thought for one second that he'd be backing off, Justin would just have to show him there'd be no backing down. No running away.

Today was only the beginning, and more of a feeling out—he almost snickered at that—of Mack's position than an all-out move to win him back. Justin had needed to see Mack, to touch him, to hear his voice and look into those blue, blue eyes. He'd needed to know that he had a chance, and how to proceed.

Tonight he'd fine-tune his plans, then tomorrow, he'd show Mack Williams just how determined he was to be Mack's man.

Chapter Five

After a fitful night of tossing and turning, Mack wasn't in the best of moods. He sent the hands out and told his foreman he felt like shit today and planned on staying around the house and tackling the mounds of paperwork that seemed to reproduce daily. Lying around in bed and moping wasn't Mack's way, but he just wasn't up to being around anyone else.

Dreams of Justin had kept him up most of the night—in more ways than one. Mack had refused to beat off again after the first time. He wasn't some dumb kid who couldn't control himself. By the time the sun had started to rise, Mack was exhausted and crankier than a calf denied a teat. Hungrier, too, as he'd skipped dinner the night before.

Mack fixed a bowl of cereal and ended up spilling most of it on himself when he drifted off while standing at the counter. "Damn it all," he grumbled, too tired to bother fixing something else to eat. He finished off the cup of warm coffee he'd been choking down, then he muttered and cursed all the way back to his bathroom.

The milk from the cereal bowl had soaked through his shirt and part of his jeans. After having worn sticky clothes yesterday, even for a short while, Mack was in no mood to do so again today. He averted his gaze when he normally would have looked in the mirror. Mack was full-up tired of himself. There was a little voice chattering away in his ear telling him he wasn't really hanging around to work, but rather because he was waiting—

"Aw, fuck that," Mack gritted out, irked to high heaven with himself. He got in the shower and scrubbed like his skin had offended him and needed to be punished. Justin was on his mind constantly, no matter how hard Mack tried to block the fucker out. It wasn't possible. In one way or another, Justin had always been with him. First as a friend, then a lover, then the man who had broken Mack almost to the point where he couldn't function.

But only almost. I walked away from him yesterday. I can do it again, not that I think I'll need to. Doesn't seem like he's coming back. Mack had honestly expected Justin to follow him inside or show up later yesterday. He was pathetic. Next he'd be looking out of his window to see if Justin was there, boom box on his shoulder, ready to blast a romantic song at him.

"Jesus, I'm a fool." Maybe he should spend the day in bed, sleeping, even if he had to knock his ass out with whisky. Even then, he'd bet Justin would slip into his dreams. Mack was already semi-hard, seemed to be his state lately unless he was full-on erect. There wasn't no soft to his dick ever since Justin had showed up.

Mack scolded himself for his lack of control as he tucked the towel around his hips. He was really going to have to find some restraint and stop thinking on Justin.

He left the bathroom and all but stomped into his bedroom, the thud of his feet on the hardwood jarring and painful in a way that satisfied some of his anger. It was almost as good as hitting someone, he mused as he glanced down.

Then a pair of boots came into his peripheral vision and Mack froze mid-step, his semi-erect dick perking right on up to stiff as a poker. Mack dragged his gaze up long, muscled legs covered in worn denim, to a bulging groin that held his attention for several long moments. He stared, transfixed, wondering if he was just imaging that dick twitching or if he was really having some effect on the man.

"Morning, cowboy," Justin drawled, pulling Mack's attention farther up, over trim hips and a narrow waist to a broad expanse of chest. Justin had his arms crossed, looking relaxed as he leaned against the bedroom doorway. His hat was tipped back and his brown eyes narrowed as he looked Mack over.

Mack didn't dare to move lest he throw himself on Justin, so he stood there, only lowering his foot back to the floor as Justin ogled him. Mack tracked Justin's gaze, following the lowering of his eyes that lingered on Mack's groin. The temptation to drop the towel was overwhelming, but Mack clenched his hand tight on the knotted-up material. His knuckles protested the increased strength, reminding him that he wasn't a young man anymore. Granted, thirty wasn't ancient, but for a cowboy, the wear and tear on a body made one feel older. Add in a broken heart, and Mack felt positively ancient sometimes.

Not that Justin seemed to think so. Mack's nipples puckered up under his intense gaze, and it was all

Mack could do not to reach up and rub at them to ease some of the tension there. It was so easy to imagine Justin walking over and licking a path down from Mack's chest to his belly button. From there it'd only be an inch or so before Justin could lick at his cock. Mack sucked in a shuddering breath and tried not to beg for Justin to do just that.

But as if he knew Mack's thoughts, Justin licked his lips, the pink tip of his tongue slicking the full bottom one and making it glisten. Justin stood up straight, pushing off the doorframe with his shoulder. He dropped his hands to his sides, and in two long strides, he was right there in front of Mack.

I don't want this. I don't want him. And I'm a fuckin' liar! Mack hated that he wanted Justin to touch him so bad, and anger once again spiked up to bubble past his lips.

"What the hell?" he got out right before Justin snapped a hand forward. There was a tug at his hips, then the towel was yanked right out of Mack's grip. Some semblance of reason must have still existed in him because Mack thought about protesting. His body apparently disagreed. When he spoke, it came out more as a plea. "Justin, please—" *Please touch me, make me feel like I'm doing more than just existing* —

A tremble worked through him, then Justin was pulling him into his arms. Mack's lips were already parted on a gasp, his entire body lighting up with want as Justin kissed him. There was nothing gentle about the kiss, nothing tentative or apologetic. Justin wasn't trying to say he was sorry with his actions, no. He was trying to claim everything Mack was, all that he had left of himself.

Mack grunted and started to push Justin away. They scuffled for a minute, then Mack realised something—

he didn't want Justin to stop. It'd been too long since Mack had felt a man inside him. That old saying about cutting off your nose to spite your face swam through his mind, and Mack thought, fuck it. He could do it, have sex without getting emotionally entangled. And if he was lucky, if he could manage it, maybe Justin would be the one who got caught up in whatever happened between them. Maybe it'd be Mack who walked away. *No 'maybe' about it. I ain't getting hurt again.*

Mack quit struggling at the same time Justin did. Mack's heart thudded and he grabbed Justin before the man could leave. He surged to his toes and crushed his mouth to Justin's, grinding every part of him that he could against that tall, muscled body.

Justin growled into the kiss and got his hands full of Mack's butt. It felt so good to have a man touching him, to feel and hear and smell arousal like this. Mack held on to Justin at his nape and shoulder, probably squeezing too hard, but Justin wasn't complaining and Mack wasn't stopping.

He turned his head enough to nip at Justin's jaw, and Justin retaliated by barrelling him backwards, Mack barely able to keep his feet as he stumbled. Justin's hold on him never loosened, not until Mack's calves hit the bed, then Mack was pushed down unceremoniously, his breath gusting out of him when he bounced on the mattress.

Justin followed him down a second or two later, finding Mack's mouth with his, the kiss almost brutal and not entirely painless. Mack didn't care. He knotted one hand in Justin's hair, knocking his hat off, and got the other hand in one of Justin's back pockets. He could feel the flexing of Justin's buttock under his palm, and Mack almost came then and there.

Justin moaned and humped, bringing friction to Mack's dick where it was pinned between them.

"Naked," Mack got out against Justin's lips.

Justin pulled his mouth away long enough to let Mack draw in air, then he was right back, mashing their lips together, tongue thrusting into Mack's mouth in a way that caused pre-cum to leak from his dick. He put his arms around Justin and pulled him as close as he could. Justin went easily, his weight on Mack comforting in a way he didn't understand.

Mack used both hands to massage the mounds of Justin's ass. He tugged and pushed, encouraging Justin to rut. Justin's clothes were suddenly unacceptable. Mack didn't want to touch anything other than Justin's skin. He jerked his head, separating their mouths.

"Damn it, bub, get your fuckin' clothes off," Mack growled. "Boots, too." The anger and pain he had felt moments ago were buried in the fiery need consuming him. Mack reassured himself that he could do this, just fuck and be done with Justin. He had to, because he couldn't stop now, and if he let Justin into his heart again — well, that didn't bear thinking on.

Justin sat up, straddling Mack's hips. He pulled off his shirt, and Mack realised he was staring all slack-jawed, but damn, Justin was cut. Before the shirt hit the floor, Mack was sitting up and putting his arms around Justin. He pulled Justin down on top of him again, lightheaded from the waves of pleasure rolling over him. Justin was pure sin in his arms, so strong and hard. He'd definitely grown since Mack had held him last, and the pelt of hair on his chest was new to him, too. Mack craned his neck and caught some of the dark red strands in his teeth. A tug on them had Justin cursing and cupping his cheek.

Mack released the hair and bucked hard, turning them over so that he was straddling Justin. He narrowed his eyes at the man and unsnapped his jeans. Justin raised his hips up and Mack scooted down until he had to get off the bed. He removed Justin's boots, along with his socks, then he peeled down those worn jeans, delighted to find Justin had gone commando.

Justin's fat cock stood up tall and proud, and Mack clenched his ass, that little hidden bud between his cheeks burning with an ache he'd all but forgotten. Mack's gaze locked on that gorgeous shaft, the slit wet with pre-cum. He lowered his head slowly, giving Justin enough time to speak up if he didn't like where this was headed.

The only sound he heard was Justin's breath hitching in his throat as his cock jerked. Anticipation made Mack's mouth water and he slid one hand under Justin's balls. His other hand he used to grip around the base of Justin's dick. Mack squeezed gently.

The urge to taste Justin was too strong to stall any longer. Mack opened his mouth and leant down. The second his tongue touched that hot, silky flesh, he moaned and looked up at Justin, needing to see his expression. Mack laved the swollen pink head and the flavour of Justin spread over his tongue. Justin moaned, his eyes crossing right before they closed. Mack had a second to feel smug then he was drawn to taste Justin again.

Mack swirled his tongue over the head again, delving it into the slit before running it under the rim. He found the little bundle of nerves on the underside and flicked it, and Justin gasped, burying his hands in Mack's hair at the same time he pushed his hips up.

Mack left off fondling Justin's balls in favour of holding the man down with a forearm below his belly, low down across his hips. He didn't care to be gagging on dick, and he wanted desperately to maintain some semblance of control.

He opened his mouth wider then and sucked half of Justin's length in, flicking his tongue over the thick veins on the underside.

"Fuck," Justin dragged out, pulling on Mack's hair. "God, I need more."

Mack came up to really worship the tip, working that spongy cap for a while as Justin began to writhe beneath him. He slid his mouth back down, his cheeks aching as he sucked harder. His lips met his hand and he released his hold on Justin's dick, daring to dive farther down that length.

Willing himself not to gag, Mack concentrated on relaxing his throat, on ignoring that uncomfortable sensation of being choked. He wanted this, wanted to blow Justin's mind as surely as he was blowing his dick. Mack swallowed and the tip of Justin's shaft breached his throat.

Justin started babbling then, pleading with him not to stop. As if Mack could. He had to taste Justin's cum, and he wouldn't give up the control he had right now, with Justin his for the taking.

"Oh fuck, fuck, Mack! Don't stop, please, fucking hell, don't stop!" Justin's hips shot up despite Mack's hold on him.

Mack growled around the cock in his mouth and pushed harder against Justin's hips. He came back up, letting his teeth drag here and there, a soft scrape that seemed to be driving Justin out of his mind. Wordless sounds left his lips, broken, gasped noises that were barely human-sounding.

Never had Mack felt so strong, so in control of not only himself but another person. He pinned Justin down but good and sucked his cock in again, this time not hesitating to go deep. When the fat crown entered his throat, Mack still had to work at not gagging, and he swallowed reflexively.

Justin shouted, and Mack shoved his hand under Justin's ass, burying his thumb in the deep seam of his cheeks. He pressed his thumb over the tight little muscle he found there, and Justin's next yell nearly rattled the windows.

It was enough warning for him to pull off, but Mack didn't, couldn't. He moved back enough to catch the first spurt of cum on his tongue, then he swallowed it along with the rest of Justin's load. The salty, bitter taste wasn't altogether pleasant, but there was something about it Mack loved, something he knew he'd crave from then on.

"Aw, shit, cowboy," Justin rasped, humping sporadically. "Think you done killed me."

"Obviously not," Mack uttered as he released Justin's cock. "You're still talking, and I need to come." He pushed himself up the length of Justin's body and took Justin's mouth in a kiss that almost had him nutting then. He needed more, though, and so he wedged his hips between Justin's thighs, bringing them cock to cock, balls to balls.

Mack groaned and clutched at Justin, not caring particularly where he held on, just as long as he was touching the man. He rocked into the warm cradle of Justin's thighs, and felt his sac draw tight. Having Justin come apart for him had pushed Mack to the edge, and it wouldn't take long for him to come. Mack thrust against Justin's cock.

"Take what you need," Justin urged, his lips moving against Mack's. "Do it, baby. Fuck me until you shoot."

Mack knew Justin didn't really mean *fuck* him, but the thought of it, of ploughing Justin's ass and pushing the anger and hurt into him with each powerful thrust, sent Mack into orbit. He rutted on Justin, purring when he felt a finger teasing at his asshole. Mack wanted to beg, wanted to ask Justin to just do it, take him and fuck the pain and pissed-off right out of him. Mack bit his lips until he tasted blood to keep the words back.

There'd been a time when Justin had known him like no one else ever had, and Mack feared very much that the same was still true when Justin flipped them over again. Justin slid between his legs, and damned if those traitorous limbs didn't part like the Red Sea for a prophet.

Mack turned his head aside, chest heaving and so many confusing emotions rushing around in him he didn't know how to sort them out. He didn't want to, to be honest, and he didn't want to think anymore.

"Where's the lube?" Justin asked, voice gravelly with want.

Mack's voice shook when he answered, but he figured he was just lucky it didn't squeak like a rubber duck. "Lube, and condoms." He stressed that last word emphatically. He didn't know who all Justin had been with, and thinking on it made him want to puke, so Mack pushed it aside. "They're both in the nightstand drawer."

Justin shifted on top of him, then Mack's chin was cupped, his head tugged until he turned to look at Justin. Was that a grimace on the man's face? And what the hell was his problem?

"We'll discuss that after," Justin said, and Mack had no fucking idea what he meant by that. He didn't care, either. He was in danger of losing the sexual high he'd been soaring on, and that just wouldn't do at all.

"Stop wasting my time with your jabbering now and just do it," he gritted out, immediately blushing afterwards.

"Do it?" Justin repeated, arching a brow at him. "You mean, fuck you?"

"Yes," Mack snapped. "What the hell is the holdup? You need more time to get up?"

"Not hardly," Justin snarled back, fisting his cock and shaking it at Mack. "Does this look like I need more time?"

Mack didn't answer, and Justin glared at him before leaning over and opening the drawer. Justin dug through it with short, sharp movements that jostled Mack and shook the bed a bit, then condoms and lube were being tossed onto the blanket by Mack's legs.

Justin sat back on his heels between Mack's thighs and grabbed the strip of condoms. He tore one off and dropped the rest, something very much like anger darkening his features. Mack tried not to gulp as he watched Justin roll the thin layer of latex down his veiny cock. He wanted that thing in him, but it surely looked too big to fit up his ass. Justin had grown all over since Mack had last seen him, no doubt.

"Raise your leg up," Justin instructed roughly, nudging Mack's right knee.

Mack just knew he was a brilliant shade of red as he hitched his leg up, exposing his hole. He felt like everything down there was magnified and put up on one of those big movie screens. No one had ever looked at him there, other than himself a few times he was feeling kinky with his masturbating.

Breaking the Devil

"Looks hungry," Justin said, an almost dream-like expression in place as he stroked wet fingers over Mack's pucker. Mack didn't even know when Justin had opened the lube. He'd been too busy being mortified and turned on at the same time. "Love seeing you on display like this," Justin continued as he massaged Mack's hole. "Pick your other leg up so you really spread open for me. Show me everything, cowboy."

Mack was just going to die, he was so embarrassed, yet he didn't hesitate — much — to pull his other leg up too. It was such a turn on, the way he felt his ass open, his cheeks part when he pulled his knees up to his chest. Damn, he wanted to see Justin like this, all slutty with need.

Pressure against his hole had Mack wincing, fear skittering up his spine even though he wanted what was happening, wanted it enough to roll his hips and try to impale himself on Justin's fingers.

"Patience," Justin said in a voice that sounded like he was anything but. Still, the way he kept rubbing over Mack's pucker, massaging it, helped Mack to relax. He hissed as one thick digit penetrated him, but the burn was almost nonexistent, and the pleasure was well worth any discomfort.

"There you go, cowboy. So silky and hot inside, so fuckin' tight," Justin muttered. "Now I know why the condom box was still unopened. Been a while, hasn't it?"

If Justin only knew. But Mack didn't want him to know anything other than that he needed to hurry up and do something to ease the ache of need building in him.

"I could make you come like this, but you're so tight already, it'd take forever to loosen you up so I could get back in."

"Then you'd better hurry up before I shoot all over the place." Mack wouldn't have been surprised if when he came he didn't squirt out twice the load he normally did. Justin was doing it for him like nothing else ever had.

Justin dipped down and without warning, bit Mack's left nipple hard enough to sting.

"What the fuck!" he yelped, his cock growing even harder.

"Goddamn, the way you clenched around my finger, you'll squeeze my dick plumb off if you don't relax some." Despite his words, Justin seemed even hornier than before. A red flush had climbed up from his torso to his neck and cheeks, proof of his arousal, and his eyes fairly glowed with the inner fire of wantonness.

Mack hitched his legs over his nipples, not sure he wanted to risk another bite. It wasn't that it hurt so much as he would come and he really wanted to wait until Justin was inside him to do that.

Justin's smirk told him the tease knew exactly what he was thinking. Mack debated flipping him off, but an increase in the pressure around his ring caused him to gasp.

"Yeah, cowboy, I'm opening this sweet ass of yours up," Justin said. "Feel me taking you, claiming this—"

Mack jolted, his neck arching as pleasure rolled up from inside him in slow, warm waves.

"Yeah, just give it up for me. I'll blow your mind, baby." Justin kept rubbing that spot inside him that was making Mack lightheaded. Sounds he wished he could keep hidden kept slipping past his lips as Justin pushed him closer and closer to climax.

Just when Mack thought he was going to come, Justin added another finger to the mix, and the pain, though not too intense, stalled his orgasm before it could barrel over him.

"Easy, easy. Relax for me. I promise I'll make this so good for you."

Mack could barely concentrate to make out Justin's words. His body was afire with a need that was all-consuming. When Justin pulled those fingers out, Mack keened in protest, his pride long gone and buried under the animalistic needs of his body.

"Hands and knees, Mack. You're tight as a virgin still, and this'll be easier for you, plus I don't want to hurt you."

Mack didn't hesitate to comply. He needed Justin in him and it occurred to him in a moment of lucidity that he'd be completely exposed if he were facing Justin. Any longing or regret that might be bared wasn't anything Justin ever needed to see. He flipped over, rising up on his knees and bending at the waist.

"Grab on to the headboard," Justin instructed. "I don't wanna slam you into it when we get going."

Mack did him one better, using the slats on the headboard to keep himself on his knees only with his torso bent but not down on the bed. He didn't want to go completely ass-up for Justin, and he didn't ask himself why.

Justin pressed a hand to his lower back and Mack arched, pushing his butt out. He slid his knees farther apart, feeling deliciously dirty as he opened himself for Justin.

"Oh yeah, cowboy, you're giving me quite a show." Justin stroked down his ass then pushed his fingers back into Mack's hole. "Shit, that's gonna feel so good around my dick."

"Then get on it," Mack urged, so horny and ready for it he couldn't hardly talk.

"Bossy," Justin muttered, then he grasped both of Mack's cheeks and pulled them apart. "And open and waiting for me."

Mack swallowed back any retort because Justin scooted up behind him. The fat, blunt tip of Justin's cock felt like a baseball bat as it spread his ring wider than Justin's fingers had.

"Jus…" Mack sputtered, unable to get the rest of Justin's name out as the burn intensified. It was the strangest thing, the way it hurt and pleasured him at the same time. Mack didn't understand it, but he didn't have to. Justin gripped him at the hip and shoulder, sinking that long shaft deeper into him.

"Better hold on, cowboy," Justin warned right before he pushed in to the hilt. A bright spark of pain tore through Mack at the sudden invasion, but it only seemed fitting to his fevered brain, and it served to remind him that letting Justin in, in any way, would and did hurt.

Justin froze, his thighs rock hard against the backside of Mack's. "Shit, shit, I didn't mean to—are you okay?"

He sounded worried, and that just wouldn't do. Mack didn't need any emotional entanglement now, on either of their parts. He just needed to be fucked until he passed out. "Get on with it," he got out, none too politely.

Justin hissed at him and withdrew so slowly Mack wanted to slap him. He didn't want to be treated like he was breakable.

All the unspoken, tangled-up words Mack had been holding in culminated into a shout as Justin's hips slammed against his ass. He couldn't tell which was stronger, the pain or the pleasure, and he didn't get any time to ponder it, because Justin withdrew and immediately thrust in again.

"Jesus...Christ..."

Justin's voice cracked and he seemed to jerk behind Mack, like he'd been poked with a cattle prod. Mack squeezed his ass, trying to get Justin to moving again, because he thought he was liking it more than it was hurting.

"Mack," Justin growled, clenching his hands where he held Mack. There'd be bruises, Mack thought, and why that made him almost giddy was beyond him.

Mack tightened his butt again and Justin made an animalistic sound that reminded Mack of a cornered wolf. Then he began fucking Mack so hard Mack couldn't do anything but try to keep his arms from collapsing so he didn't get fucked into the headboard.

"Tried to warn you," Justin was saying as he hammered away at Mack's ass. "You just wouldn't...let me..."

Mack thought the word 'control' got mumbled, but he wasn't sure. It was hard to hear over his own raspy panting and slap of Justin's flesh hitting his.

Mack stiffened his arms and arched a little more. The effect was instantaneous, bringing Justin's dick into contact with Mack's prostate. "Goddamn," Mack huffed out as lightning bolts of pleasure shot up to his nipples, making them ache for a touch.

Justin thrust even harder, burying his cock so deep inside Mack he didn't know why he wasn't tasting it. Passivity wasn't in Mack's nature, and he rammed himself back into every thrust, fucking himself on Justin's dick as surely as Justin was fucking him. With his gland being stimulated repeatedly, Mack was fuzzy-headed with the impending release. He was soaring, his body light and heavy with lust at the same time. His fingers and toes tingled like they were just waking up, and his cock was dripping pre-cum steadily.

He thought he heard Justin laugh, a strange, wonderful sound that caused a round of butterflies to take off in Mack's belly. *No. None of that shit. It's just sex, just fucking. Can't be more.* Justin reached under him and fisted Mack's dick, and Mack forgot to worry about what he might be feeling other than that hand on his cock and Justin's shaft in his ass.

Faster and faster, Justin fucked him until Mack's arms were shaking from the strain of supporting his weight. He cried out, so hungry to come he couldn't keep silent, and Justin loosed another laugh.

"Come for me, cowboy. Come with me, 'cause I can't hold back any longer."

The words alone caused another wave of heat to spread through Mack, coiling low in his belly and clamping his ass down on the cock inside. He tensed and tightened every muscle he could, and bellowed as cum shot up his dick.

Justin's shout cut off as he shoved in deep and held still. Then he moved in small undulations, panting as he came.

Mack's right hand slipped when the next spurt of cum jetted from his slit. He gave up trying to remain somewhat upright and fell forward, spilling the rest of his climax onto the blanket. It felt wrong for Justin to pull out, like he was taking part of Mack with him, and damn it all to hell and back, Mack closed his eyes against a sting he knew threatened to turn into tears.

Jesus, what kinda man bawls like a baby after sex? He feared he was about to find out. Twelve years of carrying around an anguish he often thought should kill him, and it was coming to a head, like a damn bursting under a torrential flood. Mack still thought he could keep it together—until Justin curled up beside him and pulled Mack into his arms.

Then it wasn't just tears from pent-up emotions, it was anger and shame, too, that had Mack shoving Justin away violently and springing up off the bed. Mack swiped at his cheeks and was surprised to find them barely even damp. He needed Justin gone before he broke down completely.

"Hey, love, please don't," Justin whispered, sounding almost as hurt as Mack felt.

Mack didn't buy it for a goddamned minute. He felt Justin's gaze on him but refused to turn back around and face him. Instead he headed for the bathroom again, stopping only at the doorway to inform Justin of something he'd obviously forgotten.

"My name is *Mack*. Not love." Justin seemed to have a problem remembering that.

A cracking noise told him that Justin was fisting his hands, popping his knuckles like he'd done so long ago when he was frustrated. Back then it had been a sign that his temper was on edge, and Mack could only assume the same held true now. He told himself he didn't care.

"I don't suppose you'd believe that they *are* the same to me, your name and love," Justin said quietly.

Even as the proclamation tried to warm his heart, and despite the hurt and hope he heard in Justin's voice, Mack couldn't hold back a sarcastic snort. "No, I don't suppose I would, seeing as how that line of shit is about a dozen years too late in coming. You need to leave, now." *I need you to leave now, before I turn around and become your fool all over again.* Mack was proud that he had kept all the emotion out of his voice, that he'd sounded as if he didn't care about Justin or what they'd once had or done a few minutes ago.

Then he heard the bed springs squeak, followed by the padding of feet on the hardwood floor. There was the sound of something splatting into his bedroom trash can, which he supposed was the condom.

Then more footsteps. Panic rushed up under his skin, making him hot with fear. It gave him the strength he'd lacked moments ago to look at Justin. Mack spun around and flung out a hand in front of himself, fingertips pointed at the ceiling. It was a flimsy barrier between him and Justin, but it sufficed. Justin opened his mouth, but Mack cut him off.

"I mean it. Leave now, or I will. Either way works for me. We fucked, got off and we're done. I ain't willing to be anything more to you than that." Mack met Justin's eyes with a steely glare he felt to the curve of his skull. *God, please make him leave before I break down*, Mack prayed. *I can't keep acting like I ain't dying inside for much longer.* He fervently hoped none of that showed in his expression, that he was as cold in appearance as he wished he could be inside.

With a curt nod, Justin turned and walked over to his jeans. "Just so you know, I'll leave this time 'cause you look like you might break if I don't," Justin said.

Mack wanted to melt right into the floor.

Justin turned around to face him again. "You need to understand something, though." Justin went still like a rattler before it struck. "You have a short—and I mean very short—reprieve. I'll be back, and you and me, we're gonna have a talk. Whether that's before or after we fuck, I can't say, but we *will* talk."

Mack should have been forewarned by the determined glint in Justin's eyes, but somehow he didn't catch on until Justin was striding back to him, still naked and gorgeous as sin. Mack opened his mouth to tell him to fuck off but Justin shot one long arm out and whipped his hand around Mack's nape. With a jerk, he had Mack stumbling into him, then Justin was kissing him, holding him with those rough hands, touching him all over and plundering his mouth.

And before Mack could gather his wits or reserve, Justin released him. Mack looked down at the floor, unable to watch Justin get dressed. There were no footsteps leading away, though, and Mack realised Justin was still there, standing in front of him.

"Go," Mack said weakly, after he'd swallowed down a knot of regret he refused to let free. He blinked rapidly and glanced to find Justin smiling at him with such tenderness Mack knew he had to have imagined it.

Justin touched his shoulder, just a soft, gentle caress then he stepped back. "I'm going, for now, but I can't stay away from you for long, Mack. I just can't, and I don't even wanna try." Then Justin nodded towards him. "Go on. I can't leave with you standing here looking like you do."

Mack didn't want to know what Justin was seeing when he looked at him, so he didn't ask and instead spun around. As soon as he stepped into the bathroom, the door was closed behind him. He guessed Justin had done it as there was no other explanation. For some reason, Mack wanted to turn around, to take back the harsh words he'd flung at Justin, but he didn't. He clamped his mouth shut firmly, refusing to let another sound out. No way would he let his mouth overrule his brain again, in any manner—word or deed.

Mack stood there for a while, resting his head against the door, listening to Justin getting dressed, the rustle of clothes being pulled on. He slid his hand over the door knob, so tempted to turn it, but he found his faltering willpower before he could give in to the impulse. Mack jerked his hand back and shook it out, like he could shake the need from under his skin. Mack was afraid that wasn't the case, that Justin was embedded in him, maybe even in the marrow of his bones, and Mack would never be free of the need for him.

Even if that were the case, there was no reason to compound his idiocy with more bad choices. He'd already behaved like a hormone-crazed slut, begging Justin with body if not words to fuck him.

Mack's ass was sore from the fucking he'd got, and he only realised it then. He clenched his ass, revelling in the sensation of having been so well-ploughed. His revelry quickly turned to disgust with himself. What was he doing? He was worse than some hearts-and-starry-eyed kid.

Don't be fucking stupid, Mack thought, then turned on the shower as he let out a bitter laugh. Oh no, he shouldn't laugh, because *Justin* had been fucking Stupid, and Stupid had enjoyed every goddamned minute of it.

Shaking his head at his own foolishness, Mack stepped under the shower spray. He tipped up his chin and let the water wash over his face, and the tears he'd held back began to fall.

Chapter Six

It wasn't easy, leaving Mack alone when he was hurting, but Justin knew he was the cause of that pain, and hanging around wasn't going to endear him any to Mack. He wished the morning had gone differently, in a way, although he couldn't regret what had happened between them.

Still, it would have been good if they'd talked first. Justin had a lot to say, and it wasn't going to be easy for him to do it. Too many years of keeping everything inside made sharing more than his body difficult—but he'd do it for Mack. Justin would turn himself inside out if he had to, would expose every fear and weakness he had if it would help him gain Mack's forgiveness, and his love.

As much as Justin wanted to believe Mack did still hold some affection for him, he couldn't. Yeah, Mack was hurt, and angry, but that didn't mean he gave a shit about Justin. He supposed Mack might want his pound of flesh, but Justin would give him more than that. He'd hand over his entire one hundred and ninety-six pounds of self for Mack to do with as he

Bailey Bradford

pleased. Anything, anything to get him back. Justin couldn't fail in this—he'd built so many of his hopes on getting Mack to love him again.

The house looked like it had when Justin had last seen the inside of it. The walls in every room were white, undecorated for the most part except for the occasional painting of some cowboy scene or another. There were no pictures of family on display anywhere, but there never had been. The hardwood floors were clean, though, and so was the rest of the house. There was just no heart to it, Justin thought. It was a place to live, not a home. He didn't think it ever had been, and wondered if Mack knew that.

He wondered if Mack had been living or just existing. Justin thought about the condoms and lube. Something cold and angry curled in his gut at the idea of anyone else touching Mack. He didn't have the right to be jealous, but he was and he couldn't seem to squash that ugly emotion.

Reassuring himself that the condom box had been unopened was a waste of time, because there was no telling how many boxes of the damned things Mack could have gone through in a dozen years. Justin was going to have to get past that whole issue, at least until they got the opportunity to discuss their sexual history. Justin planned to skirt the details. He didn't want to know how many lovers Mack had been with, but they both needed to make sure they were safe.

Justin took one last look around the house, his ears perking up when he heard the shower start. Mack would be naked, wet and soapy under the spray—

"Cut it out, horn dog," Justin chastised himself. His dick didn't listen, and he sighed. It was going to be another uncomfortable ride back to his place.

Minx was outside, tied under the shade tree. There was grass for her there, patches of it, at least. The Texas drought was likely going to kill that off too. There weren't many plants that could live through the God-awful heat and lack of rain. Mesquite and scrub, cactus and those fucking grass burrs that nothing seemed to kill. They were about all that'd be left in another couple of months if they didn't get some rain.

Justin murmured soothingly to Minx as he approached. The mare wasn't easily spooked, he just liked talking to her. Fact was, she was about the best friend he had right then. Craig was okay, but they were buddies, and obviously not exactly close considering what they hadn't known about each other.

"D'you have a good snack?" Justin asked Minx, rubbing her neck then scratching behind her nearest ear. "Yeah, you been chillin' out here, haven't you?"

He untied her reins and mounted up. "Home again, baby girl."

His erection had subsided enough that the ride didn't cut off his circulation or anything, but the morning was already hot, and he was soaked in sweat by the time he got home.

"Want me to take care of Minx?" Craig asked, coming out of the barn. "I just finished organising the tack room. Got the order in from Flance's and don't think there's anything else we need for the horses. I've got some time before I plan on heading out to check the north field."

Justin blinked stupidly for a second, his mind racing to leap from thoughts of winning Mack's heart to the business of ranching. "Yeah, if you don't mind. I need a shower myself." The sweat he could handle, but the scent of Mack on his skin was going to make it difficult for Justin to get anything done unless he washed it off.

Craig gave him a knowing look and held his hands out for the reins. "Don't look like your fella is keen on being won over."

Justin didn't care just then how deadly dangerous Craig was. He glared at the bigger man and dismounted. Justin handed the reins over, but didn't release them when Craig tried to take them. "Mack is mine, Craig, just to be clear. He might be kicking and pawing the ground at me, but he's mine just as surely as it's hot in Texas right now."

Craig didn't look intimidated in the least as he said, "Not that I'm wanting this guy — I don't know what he looks like, and even so, he sounds like too damned much work for me — but regardless, he might not want to be yours. That's something you're gonna have to deal with, if it's so."

Justin couldn't reply, because he'd only have been able to tell Craig to go fuck himself, followed by firing him. He turned on his heel and strode across the dusty yard and up the porch steps.

Once he was inside, the cooler air from the air conditioning helped cool Justin's temper. He still wanted to knock the shit out of Craig, even though he understood what the ass had meant. Justin didn't like it, but he had to admit there was a chance Mack hated him too much to ever forgive him.

No, he didn't have to admit that. Justin wouldn't start giving such a thought credence, because he firmly believed that if you kept your goal in mind, and had confidence in yourself — and in this case, Mack — then you'd be able to attain whatever goal you were trying to reach. Negative thoughts led to negative actions, and if you weren't careful, you'd undermine yourself just because you'd kind of brainwashed yourself to do so.

Therefore, no thinking about failing, because he would not fail. Mack...he'd had such a generous heart years ago, there had to be some of it left underneath the veneer of anger and aloofness Mack tried to maintain.

Justin closed his eyes, stopping in the hallway and moaning softly as he thought about Mack, his skin slicked with sweat, driving that sweet, round ass back again and again as Justin fucked him. That hadn't been just sex, no matter what Mack tried to claim. Mack had felt it, too, the need, the connection between them. It was that connection, not the physical act itself, which had made their love-making so hot. It'd been borderline brutal, hot and harsh, but there'd been so much feeling between them...

Justin's cock was hard again and he snorted, amused at himself. He opened his eyes and went into the bathroom. It didn't take him long to clean up, and he steadfastly refused to beat off. His climaxes would all be for Mack now, and he wouldn't have to wait long for release. Neither would Mack, because they were drawn to one another with an invisible twine of memories and affection neither were going to be able to deny.

Justin didn't want to deny anything, but he knew full well that going in and telling Mack he loved him, had always loved him, would get him nothing more than laughed at. Well, and maybe tossed out. And punched.

It was the truth, however, and with that love, he found a few more grains of patience. He'd give Mack a little time, as much as he could stand. Justin didn't know how long that'd be, but he didn't think it'd be long at all.

* * * *

Mack stood talking to Leo, his foreman, about the fence repairs the ranch hands had finally finished with. "They can take the night off, go to town and hit up the bar if they want. Hell, you can give some of them the weekend off, unless you think there's enough work to keep everyone busy," Mack said after listening to him ramble on.

Leo tipped his hat back and spat a gob of tobacco juice on the ground. Mack scrunched up his nose, trying not to lose his lunch. It didn't matter how often he'd seen it done, that shit always made him queasy. It wasn't the spitting, either, but the snuff itself. It always reminded him of his dad, a cold, angry man if ever one had lived.

"Yeah, I reckon we can let Sam and Clancy take the weekend off, probably Rusty, too. That'll leave you, me and Hank here. Should be fine."

Mack averted his gaze as he saw Leo puckering up for another spit. He had to swallow back bile before he spoke, and he might have sounded a bit disgusted when he did so. "Why don't you take the weekend off, Leo? You haven't been to that big church you like in San Antonio for a while. You could go Saturday and stay over, take in the Sunday services if you want." Mack didn't much care for church, and his soul—that was something he and God would deal with, not anyone else. He couldn't say why he wanted Leo gone, except that the man had been around too much lately. Honestly, Mack had thought Leo would leave when Mack's dad had died, but that hadn't been the case.

"Church would be a good thing for your soul too," Leo began. Mack tried not to roll his eyes, but when Leo didn't say anything else, Mack looked at him to see what the problem was.

Leo stiffened up like something prickly had crawled up his ass, and not in a good way. Glancing over his shoulder in the direction Leo was glaring, Mack saw Justin dismounting from a pretty mare. Justin settled her in the shade then headed their way.

Yup, as sure as the sun had risen in the morning, Mack's cock started hardening right up as he watched the smooth rolling motion of Justin's hips. Mack had been left alone yesterday, and he'd fucking hated that he'd wanted Justin to show up again. Now Justin was there, getting closer with each stride of those long legs, and Mack wanted to do a happy sort of wiggling, like a dog when its owner came home. He just wanted to shake all over with joy, and that pissed him off.

It didn't kill his erection at all, though, and Mack couldn't hide it without making the swollen bulge even more noticeable. At least he didn't think Leo had caught on. That man was too busy trying to glare Justin to death to notice Mack had sprouted wood.

Justin pushed his hat up enough that Mack could see his eyes and the anger burning hot in them as Justin's gaze clashed with his. Mack turned back around and muttered to Leo, "Behave." His foreman was looking fit to be tied, which was odd. Sure, Leo was one of the few people he kind of called friend, and the only one he'd ever confided in about what had happened with Justin.

Mack regretted telling him, but there'd been no one else, and Leo had seemed sympathetic at the time.

Then he'd started in about hell and damnation and Mack had tuned him out right quick. Even with Leo's opinion about homosexuality, the foreman's look of indignation and hate seemed extreme. Mack nudged him lightly and repeated his order.

"You're the boss," Leo said, not bothering to keep his voice down as Justin approached. Mack turned to stand beside Leo, figuring it was the best place to be in case he needed to grab him and keep him from trying to beat the living daylights out of Justin. That would result in Leo getting his ass kicked to hell and back, without a doubt. Mack tugged his hat down low over his eyes, hoping the shadow the brim cast would give him some help in hiding his feelings.

Mack nodded at Justin in greeting. "Justin." That was about the best he could manage with an audience. Another part of his body wanted to greet Justin in an entirely different way, audience or not. Silently cursing his body's response to the redhead, Mack fought the urge to smack his cock into submission.

Justin walked right up to him, stopping closer than what was appropriate for friends—or enemies, which was what they were, Mack reminded himself. Leo bristled, puffing up like a little rooster, and he started to push between them. Justin's vicious look didn't seem to intimidate Leo at all, but Mack didn't want to have to find and train a new foreman. Leo drove him nuts sometimes, but Mack was used to him. He grabbed Leo by the elbow and pulled him back. "No, Leo, it's fine. Justin and I need to talk since he now owns the JMR." Mack had thought that might distract Leo. He was wrong.

"Why the fuck did you buy that place? You don't know shit about ranching," Leo sneered. "You spent all those years in the military, not raising horses and running a working ranch. I bet your foreman has to wipe your ass for you as well as run the place!"

Leo, for all his talk about church and the Bible, had one of the worst mouths Mack had ever heard. He didn't understand the reasoning Leo applied to it, and now wasn't the time to brood on it.

Temper flashed in Justin's eyes, but before Mack could get too worried, Justin banked that anger.

Mack wasn't quite sure what to make of that. Justin's temper used to go off like a powder keg. *Who would have thought Justin would ever grow up with so much control?* Mack mused. *Probably something the military drilled into him.* Mack wasn't entertained by that when he realised a lot of things about Justin had probably changed.

Justin grinned at Leo, a not altogether nice smile, and he leaned his head down closer to the short foreman. "Well, here's the thing, Leo. I bought it 'cause I wanted it, for many reasons. Now I can tack on pissing you off to that list, so there's a bonus I hadn't thought of until now."

"Fucker," Leo spat out. Mack was confused by the contempt in Leo's voice, the hate pinching his already pinched features. Leo had always reminded him of a skinny pig, if that made any sense. Small beady eyes and a snub upturned nose didn't do Leo any favours.

Justin's smile vanished and he gave Leo a scathing look. "Not that it's any of your fucking business, Leo. Nothing I do is. You'd do well to remember that. I'll give you this round, 'cause I'm thinking maybe the sun has baked your brain. Otherwise, you'd think twice, then think again, before trying to start a fight with me."

Ah, there was that temper of Justin's. For some bizarre reason, it only made Mack's dick harder. *Jesus, I gotta be one bent fucker.*

Leo started to surge forward, and Justin stepped up to meet him. This time, Mack shoved himself between the two of them. He was wedged in sideways, and he extended his arms, his hands planted against each man's chest. Mack pushed them apart, grunting a bit because getting Justin to move was like shoving at a goddamn buffalo trying to run over him.

"Enough with the chest-thumping already! Leo, cut it out. Justin, rein it in and back off. We don't need this pissing contest happening, especially not with all the hands loitering around watching." He tacked that last part on in a whisper he didn't think would go any farther than the three of them. He figured his crew didn't know he was gay, though if they found out he didn't really care at this point. Anyone that had a problem with it could quit. Even so, he still would rather they not find out like this, with two idjits squabbling about him.

Mack turned his head to glare at Leo, who finally nodded. The foreman stepped back, his normally thin lips pressed so tight together Mack couldn't even see a hint of their chapped surface. Leo darted a hateful look at Justin, then pivoted away.

"Better not be any lazybones standing around here," Leo barked out. "If you ain't got enough chores to do, I can sure enough find more, boys!" The other cow hands scattered like fleas off a dead dog. Leo stomped off, boot heels striking the ground with every step. Puffs of dirt floated up from the force of the impact. Leo cussed and muttered as he made his exit. Mack gave a mental eye roll then faced Justin.

Justin stood still, nostrils flaring, and why that turned Mack on was a mystery he didn't care to examine. Justin's expression could have been chiselled from the hardest stone, anger and something darker, something very much like hate, giving Justin an almost feral appearance. Mack wondered what the hell his problem was now.

Justin didn't keep him wondering for long. "Is he the reason, cowboy?" Justin asked, pinning him in place with a piercing stare.

Mack just looked at him, arching an eyebrow in question. He thought he knew where Justin was going with this, but wasn't positive and didn't want to make a fool of himself if he was wrong. Silence was his best option for now.

Justin curled his hands into fists and popped his knuckles. He narrowed those brown eyes of his even more, until Mack didn't know how he could possibly see from them.

"The condoms in your nightstand," Justin gritted out, his mouth not opening any wider than his eyes. "Is he the reason for them? Have you been getting some from the foreman, giving that sweet ass of yours up to him?"

Mack blanched and almost laughed in surprise at Justin's misguided questioning. "Jesus, he's my foreman and kinda a friend, sometimes, Justin. Not my fuck buddy." Mack did laugh then, although he made sure to keep it low so as not to alert Leo to his amusement. The last thing he needed was for Leo to get all fired up again because he thought Mack was laughing at him. He wasn't, but the idea of the two of them...that was just crazy talk.

"And before you can ask any other dumb questions, I'd advise you to think long and hard. There's nothing

I owe you, no explanation, not a second of my time. You got all from me you'll be getting yesterday." Mack's ass was still sore, in the most delicious way. He clenched his ass just to feel the sting of it.

Mack walked towards the house, knowing Justin would follow, because the man was nothing if not tenacious. He wouldn't be letting the whole condoms-in-the-nightstand thing drop until he got an answer for why they were there to begin with, no matter what Mack told him about it not being his business.

It gave him a thrill he figured had to mean he was fucked up when Justin did indeed follow him. Mack shivered before he could stop himself, his cock growing erect as he bounced up the porch steps. He'd swear he could feel the heat from Justin's body behind him.

Justin reached around him and pulled the front door open. As he did so, he also put his other hand on the small of Mack's back, right above his belt. Justin rubbed that spot, and though it felt good, Mack walked past him. He couldn't let Justin keep touching him or else he'd roll over and beg for it.

Justin dragged his hand over Mack's hip. He followed Mack inside and shut the door.

Mack turned around, ready to explain again that nothing about him was Justin's business. He blinked as Justin moved so swiftly he was almost a blur. Justin caught him at the waist and pulled him in tight. Mack gasped, feeling that incredibly sexy body against his, then Justin began walking forward, still holding him.

Mack clutched at Justin's hips in return and stumbled backwards. He smacked into the wall, knocking his cowboy hat to the floor. "Justin—" he got out right before losing his train of thought when Justin rotated his hips, bringing their cocks together with a friction that then drew moans from both of them.

"One day, you're gonna ride me wearing nothing but that hat and a smile," Justin growled.

Oh, damn. Mack forgot about all the reasons he should be telling Justin to get the hell away from him as Justin cupped his nape and kissed him. Mack parted his lips, too eager and horny and aching for this man to deny either of them this pleasure. He bit and nipped Justin's lips, thrusting his tongue to parry Justin's.

Justin made another of those ball-emptying sounds. How Mack kept from coming all over when he heard it was beyond him. He got his hands between them and pressed his palms over Justin's tits. He could feel the hard nubbins through Justin's denim shirt.

"Fuck," Justin rasped, jerking his head aside. Mack grinned and pinched Justin's nipples, hard. "Ah! Fuck yeah!" He rutted against Mack, and began nibbling down his jaw. When he sucked at a spot right beneath Mack's ear, Mack's vision blurred as a wave of desire rolled over him. Justin wedged his hands between the wall and Mack's ass, and he kneaded his cheeks roughly.

Sensation zinged to Mack's pucker, bringing to vivid relief flashes of Justin fucking him. He moaned and tried to keep playing with Justin's nipples, but concentrating was difficult when he wanted to beg for another fucking.

"Tell me who those condoms are for," Justin whispered before taking Mack's mouth once again for a brief, fierce kiss. He continued thrusting his hips, rubbing their cocks together, each time they made contact sending bolts of heat from Mack's balls to his belly. "Tell me, cowboy. Who's been tapping this sweet ass?" Justin squeezed hard, and Mack choked when he tried to swallow. He coughed and Justin did it again. "Tell me."

"Jesus," Mack panted, "they were a gag gift from my crew on my birthday, that and a blow-up sheep, okay? You happy now?" Mack figured his humiliation was complete, and even with all that handsome man all over him, his desire ebbed a bit.

Justin froze, his tongue wet and tantalisingly close to Mack's ear for a second before he moved back and burst out laughing.

Mack scowled at him and tried to get away from the braying ass, but Justin wasn't having it, caging Mack in place with a hand on either side of his neck. He thumbed the sensitive skin beneath Mack's earlobes, driving goose bumps down Mack's spine.

Justin pressed his forehead to Mack's, staring into his eyes. "Your crew bought you a blow-up sheep? Ah, God…" Justin started laughing again, and his eyes crinkled at the outer corners. Instead of getting mad this time, Mack went warm and melty inside. Justin sounded so happy, so reminiscent of the young boy who'd been Mack's friend first, then his lover. The man might have aged, but that laughter had Mack thinking the boy he'd loved was still somewhere inside Justin.

And before he knew what he was really doing, Mack leant forward, taking that smiling mouth, kissing Justin because he wanted to share that joy, to swallow it up while Justin glowed with happiness.

A kiss meant to be an innocent celebration of laughter quickly turned into a frenzy of limbs and groans as they fought to get their clothes off.

"Gotta taste you now," Justin mumbled, sliding down to his knees. He cupped Mack's balls and Mack spread his feet farther apart as he rested his hands on Justin's shoulders. Every bit of spit in his mouth dried up in anticipation of feeling Justin sucking him in. He couldn't imagine how it was going to feel, then he didn't have to bother trying because Justin parted his lips and took half his dick into the most perfect wet, warm place.

Mack threw back his head and groaned, his eyelids sliding shut and sparks flickering to life behind them. Threading his fingers through Justin's soft hair, Mack began thrusting. Justin took him without protest, moans slipping out from Justin's mouth around Mack's dick.

Those sexy sounds were as irresistible as the building ecstasy. Mack tipped his head down and opened his eyes, needing to see Justin. It surprised him to see Justin staring up at him, saliva dripping from his mouth, his lips stretched wide around Mack's girth.

Mack thought he'd never seen a hotter sight in his entire life. Porn sure as hell couldn't compare. He wanted to take Justin, to claim him in some elemental way...

Justin made a rumbling noise and sucked hard, taking Mack into his throat. Mack yelped at the sensation of slick, wet muscles contracting around his length. He bucked and couldn't hold on any longer.

He started to come, his nerve endings lighting up with an exquisite feeling that made his head feel as if it was full of helium. Yet he had a goal, a thought he held onto. Mack pulled his hips back, leaving a spurt of cum on Justin's tongue. Then he had it, the freedom to do what he saw in his mind's eye.

Mack withdrew his cock completely and fisted it. He aimed so his next spurts of jizz splattered on Justin's chin and neck. Seeing his cum on that tanned, freckled skin prolonged his climax, giving him a couple of extra jets of spunk he'd not normally have had. At least it seemed that way, as if he came longer and harder than ever before.

"Fuck," he muttered, giving in to his weak knees then and sliding down the wall until his ass hit the floor. He swallowed once he got enough moisture in his mouth to do so, then he croaked, "Damn, you about killed me."

Justin cupped his chin and kissed him forcefully, making Mack's head spin. He left Mack plumb breathless when he stopped suddenly and spoke. "Bedroom, now. If you can't walk, I'll just have to carry you." Justin stood and pulled Mack up, too. "Move it," he grunted. "We need to get to that nightstand in a hurry. My dick's so hard I could use it as a weapon."

That was kind of what Mack was worried about, only it wasn't Justin's dick that was a danger, but the whole man himself. And Mack was afraid he was going to lose his heart completely this time. Then he'd be utterly shattered when Justin left him again.

Chapter Seven

Justin ran his fingers through the cooling cum on his neck. He looked Mack square in the eyes and licked his fingers clean. Mack's wide-eyed shock was erotic as hell, and Justin wondered how much experience the man had had. Twelve years was a long time. Mack could have made a hundred or more trips to Austin or San Antonio and got fucked—Justin couldn't think about that, or he'd go crazy. He'd always known he could be jealous and possessive, but he'd never really comprehended what that meant exactly until then.

"You can't do shit like that"—Mack gestured at the general area of Justin's head—"that sucking fingers and sucking my dick then expect me to walk. Jesus, I'm about feeling like a human-shaped Jell-O Jiggler."

Justin snickered at that. "I'd eat you up all over again if you were," he teased. It felt so good to joke with Mack. Their friendship was what he'd missed most, not the sex, although that was turning out to be pretty phenomenal. So good, he was about ready to beat off to get some relief, but that wasn't what he wanted—what he needed. Only Mack could ease Justin's itch.

"Hurry, Mack. I need you." Justin didn't have a problem admitting it, either. "Get the stuff from the bedroom, or let's both get in there on that bed of yours." He stroked his dick, grunting when Mack followed the movement with his eyes. Justin was uncomfortably hard, his cock leaking beads of pre-cum from his narrow slit. As Justin stared at him, Mack's dick sprang to half-mast. Mack fisted it and with a couple of pumps was once again fully erect.

"Bedroom," Justin reiterated. He wanted Mack so intensely he could hardly think.

Mack winked at him, cocky and handsome and stealing what bit of Justin's heart he didn't already hold. He turned and headed for the bedroom.

Justin was right behind him, so close his dick poked at Mack's buttocks once or twice. He touched Mack with his hands, too, revelling in the strong, muscular back and soft, pale skin. Mack's farmer's tan was a thing of beauty in Justin's eyes, a sign of the hard work and dedication it'd taken Mack to keep the ranch going. His admiration for Mack grew by the minute, much like his desire.

As soon as Mack got the door open, Justin locked his arms around that trim waist. He marched Mack to the bed, stopping at the side of it while Mack chuckled, obviously amused by something—most likely Justin's desperation. That was all right, Justin liked hearing Mack's laugh.

But he liked the way the man tasted too, so he let go of Mack's waist and turned him around, kissing him as soon as they were lined up well enough to do so. Justin thrust his tongue in, deep and hard, claiming Mack's mouth as his own.

When Mack melted against him, clinging and moaning for Justin, he spun Mack around and gripped him at the shoulder and waist. "Down, cowboy. Let me get the stuff."

Mack started to kneel beside the bed. Justin stopped him. "Uh-uh. Knees, Mack. Mine don't do so well on the hard floor." Not the way he planned on fucking Mack, anyways. They'd both have battered kneecaps.

"Okay," was all Mack said, then he bent and spread his legs wide as he lowered his upper body to the mattress. He stopped with his shoulders about six inches from touching the bed, supporting himself with his forearms braced on the mattress. "Good?"

Justin couldn't even answer as he ogled Mack's balls hanging low and heavy between his thighs. His cock came into view when Mack tilted his hips, and a string of pre-cum was dangling from the tip. Justin looked from it to the pink pucker exposed by Mack's position. He remembered how hard he'd fucked Mack yesterday and stroked a finger over that swirled skin.

"Are you too sore for this?" he asked as Mack flinched.

Mack looked over his shoulder and frowned, his eyebrows drawing nearly together over his nose. "Hell no. I ain't gonna break, bub. Just make sure to lube me up good and start slow."

Which meant he was sore, but hopefully not overly so. Justin would see how Mack handled being prepared, and if it was hurting the man, well, there were other things they could do.

There was one thing he wanted, needed, to do that might be too much for Mack, and it'd be best if he could get Mack to lie down. Mack would likely figure that out right quick.

Justin knew he wouldn't want to stop once he got started, so he plucked the condoms and lube out of the drawer. The lube he set on the bed, and the condom he put on as soon as he got the package opened. That taken care of, Justin bent over Mack and began kissing his cheek, his jaw then that lovely stretch of nape.

Mack gasped and squirmed as Justin sucked on the knobby bend of his neck, bringing up a purple mark. Seeing it made Justin's cock impossibly harder, and he rubbed it against Mack's buttocks. With the lubed condom, he slid around all right, but it wasn't anything like fucking the man.

He worked his way downward, placing kisses all over Mack's pale skin. Every vertebra was given some lovin' because Mack moaned and writhed when Justin paid such attention to it.

By the time he reached the dimples above Mack's ass, Mack was begging him to hurry, but Justin couldn't. He laved over each of those indentations at the same time he spread Mack's cheeks apart.

Mack shook all over, and Justin pressed a hand to his lower back. This time Mack went down onto the bed without a qualm, pillowing his head on his arms.

"Are you—" Mack started, only to yelp when Justin began licking his ass, kissing and nibbling on one cheek then the other. Mack hitched one leg up, opening himself beautifully for Justin.

Justin wasn't a fool—now, though he surely had been for too many years. He started at the top of Mack's crease and tongued that lightly-fuzzed crevice until he reached the knotted muscle he sought.

"Please, please, please," Mack chanted. "Jus, please."

Begging wasn't necessary, Justin wouldn't leave Mack hanging now. Still, hearing how much Mack needed him was a balm to Justin's soul. Even though it was only for sex, at least Mack needed him for something. Justin would take it, and hope it led to more need, more want and eventually, the love and affection he craved from Mack.

"I've got you," he whispered, then he licked that little pucker again and again. Mack's thighs trembled, his ass clenching and that ring fluttering as Justin rimmed it. He pushed Mack's cheeks farther apart, stretching his opening until it gaped, then Justin slid his tongue into the small gap.

Mack shouted like he was being pounded good. He rocked his hips, almost bouncing on the bed. Justin clamped an arm down over his lower back and stepped up his speed, tongue-fucking Mack like he longed to fuck him with his dick.

Justin could have kept at it for hours, but Mack's pleas were growing more stringent, his thrusts back more forceful. With one last, long lick, he rose up and grabbed the lube. Justin popped the cap open and squirted some of the slick in his hand.

Mack scrambled to get his knees underneath him, and he pushed his butt right up for Justin.

"Nice, baby," Justin crooned as he rubbed the lube over Mack's hole.

"Probably wet enough without that stuff," Mack said in a thin voice. "Just come on already!"

"I am, but I can't hurt you."

Mack's snort kind of dimmed some of the enjoyment Justin was feeling, along with dousing his desire a bit. He knew he deserved that doubt, though, and so he told himself to buck the fuck up and stop being an overly sensitive idiot.

"Mack," he sighed as he lined his cock up to enter paradise. Nothing more, just the name of the only man who'd ever be able to claim Justin's heart.

Justin pushed in slowly, as much for Mack's ease as for his own pleasure. The tight, hot squeeze of Mack's ring was incomparable, forcing all thoughts and regrets from the forefront of Justin's mind. He closed his eyes and tipped his head back as he sank his cock deeper into Mack's ass, his balls already drawing up in preparation of Justin's impending climax.

Biting his lips, making it hurt so he was distracted from the perfect grip of Mack's inner muscles around his cock, Justin thrust the final few inches in.

"Aw, yes," Mack hissed, wiggling his hips. "God, bub, that feels so fucking good."

"Gonna feel even better," Justin got out before withdrawing fully. He slid right back into that welcoming heat and Mack keened thinly, rocking back to take him in. "Yeah, cowboy. Buck for me."

"I so will," Mack muttered right before moving forward. Justin opened his eyes then grabbed onto his hips and Mack slammed back against his thighs. "Oh, yeah…"

Still holding back, Justin began hammering Mack's ass, fucking him as hard as he dared. Mack growled at him and shoved back with more force, demanding everything Justin had.

"Stop teasing me," Mack snarled, and Justin let the last of his restraint fly out of the window. He did some growling and snarling of his own as he held Mack tighter. Mack's legs shot out from underneath him and he slid up the bed. Justin didn't let him go, toppling down with him.

Mack got a leg hitched up and Justin followed it with one of his, framing Mack in. He ploughed into Mack's ass over and over, licking stripes over his neck and cheek.

Mack's inner walls contracted and massaged Justin's length so perfectly he never wanted to leave that warm embrace. He shoved in deep and ground against Mack's buttocks, driving a hungry sound from Mack's lips.

Then those muscles clenched so tight Justin's breath was sucked from his lungs. He shouted, throwing his head back and going blind with the strength of his climax as it tore through him.

It felt like he poured a year's worth of cum into the condom as he gasped and thrust with tiny, sharp movements. Mack's ass was just clamping and milking his cock so well Justin thought he'd die from the pleasure of it.

Mack humped the bed like his life depended on it, moaning through his own climax. Eventually they both stilled, except for their heaving chests. Justin carefully pulled out from Mack's ass then rolled onto his side and slid the condom off. He tied it and dropped it beside the bed, reminding himself to toss it later and wipe up that spot.

He wanted to hold Mack, to cuddle with him and just love on him without the need for sex between them. The idea that Mack would reject him, that he would tell Justin to get the fuck off him, kept Justin from doing so.

However, the swells of Mack's ass were irresistible. Justin ran a hand over them, not meaning to stimulate Mack or himself, only wanting to touch the man. He hoped Mack wouldn't object, and he didn't, which eased some of the tension knotted up in Justin's chest.

Maybe Mack wouldn't freak out on him or shoot poison words at his heart if he scooted a little closer. Justin did so in the tiniest increments he could manage, until he was pressed against Mack's side. As still and quiet as Mack was being, Justin wondered if he was asleep or playing possum.

Mack didn't object at first, but as soon as Justin dared to start trailing his fingers over the planes of Mack's back, Mack rolled away. Justin guessed that answered his question—Mack had been faking sleep, probably hoping Justin would leave.

Justin kept his sigh to himself, along with the pangs of regret searing through him. He sat up instead and waited until Mack looked at him, which didn't take but a few seconds. He wished he could tell what Mack was thinking behind that expressionless mask he had in place. Justin decided to take a chance and see if he could get Mack to agree to let him hang around a while longer.

"I think maybe we need to shower before we wind up stuck together on the sheets." Justin glanced down at his still-wet and shiny dick. "It sucks having to lose skin when this gets stuck to my jeans."

Mack's surprise was evident in the way his dark eyebrows arched and his short bark of laughter. "Well, I suppose we could get clean. I'm kind of cum-slicked myself."

He was, and it was erotic as hell seeing him with cum smeared over his belly and clumped in the dark hair at his groin.

"Looks good on you, though," Justin rasped out before getting up and putting on what he hoped was a charming smile. "So, let's see if we can survive being naked, wet and soapy together, huh?" He held out a hand to Mack, his heart pounding with the fear that Mack would reject it, reject him.

Mack frowned at him. "It ain't surviving a shower that worries me," he said, sending Justin's hopes plummeting. Justin started to lower his hand, but

Mack snatched it up almost too forcefully. He turned his beautiful blue eyes on Justin, and for the first time since seeing Mack again, Mack didn't seem to be trying to hide any of his feelings from Justin. There was anger in those eyes, and hurt, too—but there was also something softer, something so close to what Justin felt for Mack that he almost swooned with relief upon seeing it.

"You said we were gonna talk, either before or after," Mack pointed out, his stare turning hard and hiding his feelings again. "If I don't like what you have to say, I want your word that you'll leave. Sell your place, or let someone else manage it, but I need you gone if I say so, Justin. I can't—" Mack stopped, took a deep breath and gulped before trying again. "Obviously, I can't tell you no, and I can't keep feeling the way I have for the past twelve years. Longer, even, but especially not with what you did. So promise me, and mean it, that you'll leave if I ask you to."

Justin's stomach twisted with fear and dread. He was afraid he might just drop to his knees and be sick, might beg and plead and grovel—which wouldn't be as bad as losing Mack forever.

Mack watched him mistrustfully and Justin ached from causing the man to doubt him so much in the first place, but what was done was done, he couldn't change the past.

He could, however, try to give them both the future they should have.

Justin nodded once, and helped Mack to his feet. "I promise," he told Mack, staring into the eyes of the man he'd loved for over half his life. "It might kill me, but I'll do whatever you need me to if it makes you happy. And you'll listen—"

"I said I would," Mack interrupted harshly. He immediately looked contrite and rubbed at his forehead as he glanced away. "Sorry. This is just—I don't know. I don't know, Justin. It's a lot, and I'm scared that you'll let me down again, and I'm scared you won't, and that might not make any sense to you but goddamnit, I can't figure out what's going on in my head."

Justin wanted Mack to listen to his heart, because he thought that part of Mack got it. He wouldn't push, though, not yet. He'd waited twelve years, he could wait just a little longer.

"Try to let it go long enough for us to enjoy a shower, then we'll deal with it as we can."

It did Justin's own heart good when Mack didn't argue.

Chapter Eight

Despite his claim earlier to Justin, Mack was afraid he wouldn't want the man to leave him alone, or even leave the area for any reason. He'd meant it when he'd said it, but a shower that had turned into an erotic interlude interspersed with bouts of laughter and shared memories from better times had got to him.

Maybe he could handle Justin being around, even if they didn't so much as speak. At least he'd know where Justin was, and that he was okay.

Maybe he'd go insane when Justin took another lover.

Maybe he needed his damn fool head examined. Mack towelled off half-assedly, watching as Justin dried off his fine form. Justin's ass was remarkable, round and firm, with deep divots on the side. Mack would bet those were deep enough that he could drink from them and quench a thirst after being out in the Texas heat.

He wondered if Justin would let him fuck him.

He wondered if Justin would be around long enough for him to ask.

Mack's stomach growled and Justin glanced over at him. "Will you think I'm stalling if I ask if we can eat first? My stomach's about to gnaw clean through my back bone, and it sounds like yours is trying to do its best bear call."

Mack snorted and tossed the towel on top of the hamper. "Like it'd be calling a damn bear? That'd be competition for food." He ran the brush through his hair then handed the brush to Justin. "Nah, I figure we've worked up an appetite. Sandwiches okay?"

Justin nodded and looked relieved, although whether it was from the offer of food or the short reprieve, Mack didn't know. He didn't ask, either.

"I'll throw on some shorts and get 'em started."

"Thanks," Justin said. "I should probably check in with Craig real quick. I didn't tell him I'd be gone for long, and I think we'll be talking for a while yet."

Mack remembered the foreman, as it hadn't been long since he'd seen Craig. That, and the man was not exactly handsome, but he exuded a power that was attractive. Mack had found himself fighting back a hard-on as he'd talked to the guy, but Craig had also kind of spooked him. The guy was just too intense.

For him. Mack paused at the bathroom door and looked back at Justin.

"Huh?" Justin mumbled as he rubbed the towel over his chest.

"Craig..." Mack wished to hell he could keep the question back, but it fair to burst from his lips. "Is he gay?" *Is he competition? Have you fucked him? Has he fucked you? How do I kill him if the answer to any of those is yes?*

Justin stopped drying off and nodded, watching him closely. "Yeah, but I didn't know that until a day or two ago. I always thought he was—I don't know. I just never thought of him in those terms, I guess. He wasn't on my radar." Justin hung the towel on the towel bar as he walked over to Mack. "There's nothing like that between us, never has been, never will be. I hope you believe me."

Mack wasn't sure what to think, but Justin seemed sincere. Of course, he didn't really know the man any more, even if they'd spent a half hour in the shower laughing over old times. Better times.

Maybe not better than today, unless he blows it. God, I hope he doesn't tell me something that's gonna make me really hate him irrevocably.

"Mack, I know you don't have any reason to believe me, but—"

Mack held up one hand. "Stop. I don't know what to think, that's true. Just let me have some time to mull it over and don't push me, okay?"

"Okay, all right," Justin agreed, averting his gaze and taking a step back. "I'll be in the kitchen in a bit, after I make that call."

It was reasonable, Justin calling his foreman. Mack reassured himself that he should believe Justin about Craig and him. It wasn't like every gay man screwed every other gay man he met. That'd be as dumb as thinking every straight man fucked every straight woman he met. Promiscuity wasn't ascribed to only one group of people, and neither was fidelity.

In the kitchen, Mack pulled the cold cuts and cheese out of the fridge. He set them on the table then went back for condiments. The bread was thick-sliced homemade yeast bread that Mack bought from Mrs Schmidt in town. Once he'd tried it, he'd never bothered with the mass-produced store-bought stuff again. Two glasses of iced sweet tea and a couple of plates, and Mack had the table set.

He heard Justin approaching, his bare feet making soft thudding sounds on the hardwood floor. Mack took a seat and started fixing his sandwich, not wanting to appear like he'd been waiting on Justin.

"Everything's fine at the JMR," Justin said as he entered the kitchen. "Your foreman was right about me not knowing a lot about ranching. I have a good crew, though. Little crew, but we'll be able to hire on more men soon, I think."

Mack finished preparing his sandwich and put the slice of bread on top. "Did you even want to be a rancher, Justin?" *Did you do it just for me?* Mack wasn't sure what he wanted the answer to be.

Justin stopped beside the table and picked up a slice of bread. "I wanted to be whatever made you happy, Mack. Is this Mrs Schmidt's? She's still alive?"

"You shouldn't be doing something you don't want for yourself, and yeah to both of your last questions." Mack gestured to the bread. "It'd be damned awkward if she was making bread from the grave, wouldn't it?"

Justin mock-shuddered. "Awkward would be an understatement. God, she must be eighty at least." He sat down and took another slice. "And to answer your — well, not question, I guess. But as to ranching, I like it well enough. There wasn't any other plan for me since the day I left but to get back to you when I could."

"And that was how many tours in the Marines?" Mack snarked, almost squishing his sandwich into nothing as he tried to hold back from punching Justin for spewing such bullshit. "Because they made you re-up however many times?" Mack shook his head. "Never mind. Let's eat before I lose my appetite." He was reluctant suddenly to bring up the past again.

What if it gave Justin an excuse to leave again—what if Mack's inability not to be a bitter, angry man about it sent Justin packing?

Justin's mouth had a pinched look to it, like he was having to seal his lips together to keep from arguing, but he went ahead and started making his sandwich rather than talking.

Mack couldn't help but feel relieved. Despite knowing he'd likely be hurt even more for it, he didn't want to push Justin away. They'd have to talk about the past, though, because he couldn't just pretend the last dozen years hadn't happened. He couldn't pretend Justin hadn't abandoned him, and he couldn't trust himself not to give in to angry outbursts over it.

He was worn out on the inside, tired of hurting to his core no matter how good Justin made his body feel. If talking made Justin leave, it would probably be best for the man to go sooner rather than later, before Mack found himself even more hopelessly entangled in his own feelings.

They ate in silence, not rushing but it didn't seem like Justin was stalling either. Mack thought he ate mechanically and he wondered if Justin even tasted the food.

When they finished, Justin pushed his chair back from the table, stood up and began clearing off their plates and glasses. "You want more tea?" he asked.

"Naw, I had enough. Do you want more?" Mack half-rose out of his seat, but Justin waved him back down.

"I'll get it." He put the other dishes in the sink, leaving his glass aside. Then he got himself some more tea and sat down at the table again. He didn't speak for several minutes, and Mack felt the tension in the air like a weight on his chest. He watched Justin from

Bailey Bradford

beneath heavy-lidded eyes, seeing the nervousness in Justin in the way he fidgeted with his glass, tracing drops of condensation down it to where it puddled around the base of it on the table.

Mack finally figured that if one of them didn't speak up soon, they might come to blows, or keel over from the stress. Taking a deep breath, he tried to think of the best way to begin. He exhaled without a better idea than the one he'd had, which was only to say, "Justin."

He watched his red-haired devil stop tracing patterns on his glass and sit up straight instead. He'd bet Justin was so taut he'd snap like a bad guitar string if he was poked. After another long moment, Justin raised his gaze to Mack's, and the expression Justin wore had Mack wanting to cry out in protest.

There, in front of him now, sat a man who looked like he'd been through the hottest fires of Hell itself. *No, he looks like he's still there, and part of his Hell is staring at his salvation, not being able to attain it.* Mack had never been anyone's salvation, but he knew in the depths of his soul, that was what he was to Justin.

A chill seeped into Mack. He wasn't fit to be anyone's salvation. He hadn't been able to fix himself after Justin left. He'd never felt complete again after that, so how was he supposed to be able to save anyone else? He couldn't, and that realisation sparked his mouth into gear.

"Why are you here, Justin? I know what you said about wanting to get back to me, but..." Mack sighed, shook his head. "Come on, man. Why did you buy the ranch next to mine, and why'd you send a foreman over to contract me to work your horses?" *Why did you run away from me? How could you do that to me? Do you know how bad that hurt?* Those questions burned to be released, but Mack refused to speak them.

Justin watched him steadily, although he had a wary look about him. Mack waited, not realising he'd curled his hands into fists until his knuckles ached from it. He willed himself to uncurl his hands as he waited, telling himself not to let anger rule him. He was about ready to get up and walk out when Justin finally spoke.

"I want you to let me tell it, Mack, let me tell it all the way through. Just, listen to me before you decide to judge me, okay? Please?" Justin's voice held a plea that Mack had never heard from the man before, and it scared the daylights out of him. Jesus, maybe he didn't want to hear what happened after all. Maybe, just knowing how miserable Justin was—because it was evident then in his eyes and manner—maybe that'd be enough.

Mack feared whatever was coming might make everything worse somehow. Either it would hurt him more, or his reaction to it would hurt Justin more. Mack had been so caught up in his own feelings, he only just now could see that Justin was hurting like he was, a soul-deep pain that time hadn't even begun to heal.

The pain he saw in Justin's brown eyes almost undid him. Mack nodded when it dawned on him that Justin was still waiting for his agreement, then he leant back in his chair, forcing himself to let go of the anger for now.

Justin leant back in his chair as well, but he didn't look away from Mack. "Okay...okay then. I was going to start at the beginning, but first I have to tell you this—I never wanted to leave you. Never."

Mack almost snorted at that, his resolve to keep his temper down almost obliterated by his disbelief. But something in Justin's eyes stopped him. It was a fierce, furious look combined with a longing that resonated inside Mack. That look could almost make him believe what Justin'd said. Mack was afraid he couldn't afford to do that, not now, maybe not ever. He was equally afraid that if he didn't, he'd lose Justin forever, like he'd thought he'd done up until that day in the yard. He couldn't stay quiet, though.

"You asked me not to interrupt, but you can't say something like that to me and expect me to sit here quietly like some...some... I don't know what. Idjit, I guess, because you did leave." Mack leant forward again, placing his palms on the table. "You left me, and never once in all this time did you bother to contact me. Not. Once." He stared hard at Justin, daring him to find a good excuse for that.

Justin sighed and ran his fingers through his red hair, causing the short strands to stand up every which way. He scratched at the back of his head then dropped his hands to his lap. "Okay, I can see where you wouldn't believe that, but it's true, and I had to tell you. Even if you don't want to hear it, even if you won't ever forgive me." Justin's voice quivered a little then he shook himself and cleared his throat before continuing. This time when he spoke he sounded slightly pissed at first. "So, if that set you off, then you probably won't believe me when I tell you that I fell in love with you long before the day we made love out by the stream, but I did."

Mack rose up out of his seat, ready to do—he didn't know what. Walk off, knock Justin upside the head, something. His emotions were all over the place, and he couldn't seem to stop them from swinging like a damned pendulum in a tornado. "You don't do what you did to me to someone you love. You don't fuck them, then blow them off as a little bit of curiosity satisfied. And you don't laugh when—" Mack's voice hitched as a sob propelled by betrayal tried to break free.

His chest throbbed with the effort it took to suppress such a humiliating thing from being released. His voice was low and mean-sounding as he stepped around the table to stand at Justin's side. He was shaking with the force of his restraint, trying not to give in to the impulse to shake the bullshit right out of the man.

"You don't fucking laugh when someone tells you they love you, when they vow to...to always...always..." Mack couldn't finish, couldn't stand there in front of this man who had so carelessly tossed him aside. He had to get away, but before he made it two steps towards the door, he heard the thud of Justin's chair tipping over then strong arms wrapped around him.

Mack struggled, trying to get away. He pulled at Justin's arms, and squirmed, but he didn't hit, couldn't bring himself to hurt Justin physically.

"Listen to me, Mack!" Justin shouted in a way that made Mack think he'd said it several times before Mack had heard him. "You promised. You've got to at least hear me out before you decide I'm the devil incarnate. Stop being a stubborn fool who'd rather wallow in his own misery than maybe, *maybe* find some happiness. Or is it just easier to keep your preconceived ideas, easier than finding out everything wasn't what it seemed?"

What the hell does that mean? Mack ran it over in his mind, but before he could ask, Justin went on talking, his voice rumbling in Mack's ear, slicing through the anger that was roaring in his head.

"Tell me, is that easier than finding out what you thought happened tore me apart just like it did you? Is it easier for you to think I enjoyed hurting you? That I haven't regretted it every goddamned minute of every day?"

"What am I supposed to think?" Mack asked, his fury dwindling into hurt as he dropped his chin to his chest. "I've never been told any different, have I? Twelve years of nothing, then you show up and want a do-over. I don't know if I can." He whispered, "Last time almost broke me, Jus. I wanted to... I didn't want to kill myself, but I didn't give a shit if I died."

Justin's hold gentled as he turned Mack in his arms. Callused fingers caressed his chin, then tilted his head up until Mack had to meet Justin's eyes. The pain he saw in that warm brown gaze reflected the pain Mack felt churning in his soul. That look alone had him rethinking his own stance on the past, and he realised that Justin was telling him the truth, not playing some cruel game of manipulation.

Feeling shaky, like he'd run for miles and his limbs were exhausted, Mack nodded. "All right. I can sit back down and at least try to listen. That's all I can promise, Justin. I got years of anger and hurt in here." Mack touched his chest, then his head. Admitting it wasn't as mortifying as he'd feared it would be. He thought they were both going to be laying themselves bare.

Justin released him and Mack walked back to his chair and sat. He didn't trust his legs to hold him up.

Justin paced a few times across the kitchen before turning to face Mack again. "Okay. I have to tell this my way, not to torment you, but because I need for you to understand me." Justin took a deep breath and exhaled it shakily. He glanced down then stared right at Mack. "I fell in love with you slowly, gently, over a period of years."

Oh God, Justin was killing him already, with that one sentence trying to heal wounds Mack needed to keep open if he was to protect himself.

"When we became friends at school, I knew right then I felt something for you, something I didn't feel for anyone else. It scared me, sure, but after a few years, it just grew stronger and became a part of me. The best part of me." Justin grinned at Mack, sending a swarm of butterflies to dancing in his belly. "What I felt for you was right, it was good. I didn't know it meant I was gay. I didn't really think about it. I just knew you were everything that made me happy, you know. Bad days weren't bad once I saw you."

Justin shook his head. "Sounds ignorant, maybe, saying I didn't know I was gay, but hell, no one here talked about such things unless it was a hellfire and damnation service in church. I didn't feel damned when I looked at you, thought about you, so I just figured friends felt like that about each other."

Mack closed his eyes, thinking this was something he really wished he'd known years ago. But he hadn't, and things were what they were. He opened his eyes and watched Justin as he continued speaking.

"We both dated girls in high school, trying to keep covers, I guess now. Back then, I thought you were into females. I didn't know you were trying to hide like I was. So I bought your cover, and you bought mine. I never did have sex with any of those girls."

Justin canted his head and Mack muttered, "Me either."

Justin grinned again. "Yeah, not hard when we both dated the Bible-thumping ones. Didn't have to worry about them being let down or pressuring us for sex."

That was true. Mack had dated the 'good girls' even when he'd had many naughty offers.

"After graduation, that summer, we started spending even more time together." Justin swiped at his chin, as if scratching an itch. "Sometimes, I thought I'd see something in your eyes, or I could feel the heat from your stare. There were what I thought at first were accidental brushes from you, hands touching me, or shoulder-bumping. Once you even pressed your thigh against mine while we were sitting on the bank of the pond fishing."

Justin smiled again, such a sweet curve of lips it stole Mack's breath. "Sure, I was doing the same things, accidentally"—Justin emphasised the word and smirked—"touching you every chance I could get. But I knew what I was doing wasn't any accident. I just didn't know if what you were doing was on purpose or not. I was so consumed with wanting you, Mack."

Jesus. Mack remembered it all in vivid, screaming detail. The sweet innocence of that first love, the seduction of a man…

Justin touched himself, running a hand from one peaked nipple down to cup his dick through his jeans. "Damn it, those memories have made me hard at least a thousand times. But enough about the good memories, those aren't the problem, right?" He let go of his bulge and brought his hands to rest on the edge of the table.

Mack watched as Justin's knuckles turned white with the strength of his grip. He wondered if it was fear, or anger, or some other thing pushing at Justin until the man became a menace to the table top.

Justin's next words knocked the concern right out of Mack.

"Someone was up on the ridge above the stream that day, Mack, and apparently they saw everything. Everything."

Mack didn't have to ask, he knew immediately what day Justin was talking about. Mack went rigid with indignation and embarrassment—not at what they'd done, never that—but at someone watching them in their most tender moments, intruding even if it was unknown by he and Justin at the time. The significance of possible repercussions wasn't lost on him, and he had a very bad feeling that he knew where this was headed.

Mack nodded at Justin, a simple gesture that he hoped conveyed his comprehension of the significance of a Peeping Tom.

"After I left you and headed home..." Justin shook his head.

Mack could hardly breathe, could hardly think. He couldn't get past the fact that someone had done something twelve years ago to drive them apart. That had to be what Justin was trying to tell him. Mack wouldn't let that be what defined the memory though, he wouldn't let it taint such a sweet experience. That day with Justin had sustained and taunted him for years.

Justin's head was lowered, in shame or pain, Mack didn't know. He looked closer and was startled to realise that there were tear tracks running down the other man's cheeks.

Goddamn, he couldn't do this. Rising up, he pushed aside his own pain. He walked over to Justin and squatted beside him before wrapping Justin in his arms.

Mack had a pretty good idea that things had gone to hell in a handbasket when Justin had got home, or sometime shortly thereafter. He was almost afraid to ask how far into hell that descent went.

He settled for murmuring soothing sounds as he held his man, not worrying about what he was saying, just the tone he was using to say it. Justin finally clasped him back so hard Mack's ribs ached for a second.

"I...I need to finish this," Justin got out. "Will you let me hold you while I do it? Please?"

Mack wanted to tell Justin it was okay, that he didn't have to go on, but he knew sparing them both the rest of the telling wasn't going to help them to get past it. "Sure, baby. It's fine." He intended to hold Justin in return, which was what he thought the man really wanted. Justin trembled before he spoke again.

"When I got home, my father was waiting on the porch. I walked up just whistling and smiling, happy down to my soul. Next thing I knew, he jerked me through the door—" Justin's voice caught on a strangled sound before he stopped talking completely.

Mack felt the shivering start then, but honest to God, he didn't know if it was him, Justin or the both of them. What he did know was that Justin's daddy had been the sheriff, and a mean son of a bitch by all accounts. In his later years, he'd been nicer, or at least acted like he was, probably because he feared Judgement Day in front of God.

But Mack could remember plenty of times Justin had shown up with bruises. Mack had wondered about them, but—*But what?* he thought. What excuse did he really have for not asking about them? Shit, what an asshole he'd been, not asking because it was simply easier not to know. Another screwed-up case of 'don't ask, don't tell'. He smoothed his hands up and down Justin's back, wishing he could take away the pain his red-haired devil was feeling.

"Justin," he said, pulling back just enough to see the man's face. When Justin still kept his head down, staring blankly at the floor, Mack brought his fingers up to tip his head up until Justin looked at him. The desolate expression in Justin's eyes had Mack's heart clutching painfully.

"Hey, it's okay. I've got you now." Mack leaned in to give Justin a kiss so tender, so sweet, that tears sprang up in his own eyes. When the kiss ended, Mack stood and tugged at Justin's hand.

Justin stood and they walked into the living room. Mack sat on the couch and pulled Justin down, surprised when the man sat on his lap rather than beside him. Then he understood why, because it was easier to hold each other, to cling, to give and receive comfort.

Mack thought his heart was going to twist right out of his chest. He'd be content to hold his lover like this all night, nothing more than the way they were just then. Justin, however, changed his thinking with five words.

"I want you inside me," he whispered, then he traced the shell of Mack's ear with his tongue.

Mack knew they hadn't talked everything out, but he also knew they both needed each other, needed to know they were both there, together. "Are you sure? Because you're upset, and I don't want you to do something you might regret later on." He was trying to be noble, which kind of sucked, but it was the right thing to do.

Except Justin wasn't having it. He straddled Mack's lap and rubbed his groin against Mack's. "I'm sure. I've dreamed of this for so long, so please—" He rutted, and Mack just had to grab two handfuls of that gorgeous butt. "Please, just shut up and fuck me."

Nobility seemed a little overrated as their mouths met in a kiss that was hotter than hell and sweeter than sin. Mack hooked one arm under Justin's thighs and supported his back with the other, keeping him close.

"Wrap your legs around me," he ordered, then he rose up and strode to the bedroom with Justin nipping and sucking on his neck. Every step he took had their dicks pressing together in a way that was absolutely sublime.

Mack struggled for control. If Justin kept it up, Mack would spurt before he made it to the bedroom. He started running numbers through his head, payments and accounts receivable, quadratic equations—and kicked his bedroom door shut behind them as he stumbled towards the bed.

He stopped and set Justin on his feet. "Strip," he growled, because, oh hell yeah, he was finally going to be in Justin.

Chapter Nine

Justin was a jumble of nerves inside. He wanted Mack to fuck him, oh God, did he want that. He'd never let anyone else have him. He couldn't, not when his heart belonged to this man.

Combined with that, he hoped...he hoped this meant Mack might forgive him, might understand what had driven him away. There was more to discuss, but later. Right now he needed to give himself to Mack. And more for Mack's sake than his own, he had to admit that he'd never been fucked. Mack would wonder if he'd hurt Justin or been too rushed if he found out later.

"Mack," Justin said, stroking the firm line of Mack's jaw. "Just so you know, I've never let anyone in me before."

Mack's eyes went wide and he squeaked, "Never?"

Justin shook his head. "Nope. I knew I was coming back to you. Always." Even if it'd been in an urn, as he'd designated in his will. He belonged to Mack.

"Oh." Mack bit his bottom lip then released it. "I, uh, I've never...you know. Topped."

Oh, Justin had questions, but he didn't have the right to ask them. Didn't mean he wouldn't, later. When he wasn't needing so bad. "Do what you like done to you," he suggested, and Mack nodded.

"Then why don't you strip those pants off, because I don't think I can wait much longer to take you."

Justin got his jeans off in a flash and tossed them aside. Mack wasn't far behind him.

"Get on the bed, on your back while I get the stuff."

Justin took a step and got one knee on the mattress. "You sure you want me face up?"

Mack stopped mid-reach for the drawer that held the supplies. He turned to Justin. "I want to see your face when I slide into that tight, beautiful ass of yours."

"Well. All right then." Justin gulped when Mack turned away. He wasn't sure how he felt about face-to-face sex. They hadn't done that yet, and he thought he knew why. There was no way to hide what he was feeling this way. But he owed Mack every bit of truth he could give him, so Justin flopped onto his back on the bed. He even decided to give Mack a show and hitched his legs up to his chest.

"Goddamn, that's got to be the sexiest view in the world," Mack said when he turned around again. His mouth hitched up on one side. "I'm gonna lick that pretty dick of yours, suck it down as deep as I can, make your eyes cross," he continued. "Then I'm gonna lick your balls, lick down your crack and eat your ass until you beg me to fuck you."

"Oh fuck," Justin rasped, feeling feverish with want. He clutched the backs of his thighs so hard he probably would have bruises. "Can you...can you do that now? I'll beg right now if you want me to."

Mack gave a sharp shake of his head, then he was kneeling on the bed. He bent and sucked on the tip of Justin's cock. Justin moaned and tried to rock deeper into that wet heat.

"Mm-mm," Mack hummed around the crown, eyes bright, appearing to be delighted in the mewling sound Justin made in response to the pleasure it brought him. He flicked the slit with his tongue, then bobbed down and Justin arched, trying again to sink deeper into that warm cavern.

Justin moaned when Mack cupped his balls in one hand. Mack rolled them, then released his nuts and used both to cup Justin's ass. Mack pushed Justin's bottom up and licked from the tip of Justin's cock to his balls. He sucked them in one at a time, kneading Justin's ass all the while.

Justin was edging closer to orgasm with each touch, each lick and suck from Mack. Sounds he'd never thought he'd make were spilling from him, and he couldn't keep still. His cock needed a touch, his tits ached and his hole — damn it, he *needed*!

Mack lapped at his nuts then pushed Justin's butt up higher. Justin stilled as he waited, then Mack pried his cheeks apart.

"Oh man, I have to—" was all Mack said before a mind-blowing lick dragged over his hole.

Justin lost all ability to be coherent, stuttering and choking on words that he couldn't quite get properly formed. Mack was making humming sounds, murmuring perhaps as he pressed his lips to Justin's hole.

Justin tried to pull his legs up more, offering his ass completely to Mack. It felt like Mack was rubbing his face in his crease, his lips and tongue pressed over Justin's pucker and his forehead on Justin's balls. The idea that Mack was doing that, rolling against him like he was some kind of treat, just about did it for Justin.

Then he felt it, the slick, damp stab of Mack's tongue piercing his hole. Justin shouted, so lost in the pleasure he didn't care if everyone in the state of Texas heard his yell.

Mack tongued him until Justin was all but sobbing for him to fuck him. Another rasp of Mack's tongue over his hole and Justin found the words to beg.

"Mack, I need...please, need you," Justin pleaded, letting go of his legs.

Mack sucked on his perineum and Justin's eyelids drifted shut as he moaned. For a man who hadn't topped, Mack was doing everything perfectly, turning Justin inside out with a raw desire that threatened to burn him alive.

He peeked through narrowly-slitted lids to see Mack lapping at his balls. Justin ran a hand through Mack's dark hair then gave it a tug. "Mack," he rumbled, trying not to give in to the impulse to drag Mack up his body. "Hurry. Stop torturing me."

"Wasn't trying to torture you, I was just enjoying this," Mack said, then he tongued Justin's balls. He didn't linger, though, rising to his knees and grabbing the condom.

Mack tore the wrapper open then took the condom out and tossed the package. He rolled the condom on, and Justin watched eagerly, admiring the length and girth of Mack's cock. The man was hung, and Justin was both eager and terrified of that thing going in his ass. As Mack slicked his shaft up with lube, Justin decided he was definitely more eager for it than terrified.

Mack ran his slippery fingers over Justin's balls, then down farther to his hole. "Man, you are so tight here," he said as he rubbed and rubbed.

Justin was growing desperate to be filled. He bowed up enough to reach Mack's forearm. "In me, cowboy, or I'll be riding a cowboy right quick."

"I'd take you up on that, but I really want to do the driving." Mack pushed a finger into him.

"Oh...oh damn." That felt like so much more than a tongue! Mack reached deeper into him. Justin gasped as his prostate was brushed over. "Again!" He understood with that first swipe exactly why a man would beg for this.

"Feels good, huh?" Mack asked, slipping another digit in. For an answer, Justin pumped his hips, trying to get Mack to touch his gland again. Mack obliged and Justin's world became a very wonderful place.

"Yes, yes, aw hell." Justin moaned and grabbed his dick at the base before he came all over himself. His balls were tight and ready to pump out his release. "Better hurry, Mack. Gonna lose it soon."

"We can't have that," Mack said in a tight voice. He withdrew his fingers then moved into place. Justin tried to help when Mack lifted his legs, but he was feeling all sorts of discombobulated and uncoordinated. He got one up on Mack's shoulder. That was as good as it was going to get at that point. Mack lined his cock up and pushed in an inch or two, stretching Justin's hole wide.

Justin panted, trying to relax, but that cock of Mack's was a hell of a lot wider than two fingers.

"Relax, push out," Mack murmured.

Justin knew that, he did, but it was totally different to be the one being told to do it than it was telling someone else to do it.

Mack petted his belly and held still while Justin fought to make himself relax. He thought of how bad he wanted Mack, how much he wanted Mack to be the only man ever allowed in him. That did the trick, and Mack lifted Justin's other leg up.

Then the magic began, with Mack sliding into him to the hilt in one long, slow glide.

"Oh!" Justin's eyes felt dry and wide as he was filled so well he couldn't imagine taking any more. He tried squeezing his ass and got a yelp from Mack for it. That, and a hot spike of pleasure that zinged up from his behind to his dick, making it leak pre-cum.

Mack ground out a wordless sound and withdrew a bit. Before Justin could beg, Mack pushed back in.

It was perfect, that pull and tug, the drag of dick against his inner walls. Justin had never had a clue he'd love being fucked as much as he was. Mack began to thrust, small movements at first, then with more force. His cock rubbed over Justin's gland more often than not, and Justin arched his back, trying to get more.

More of Mack, more of the slowly spreading ecstasy heating him from the inside. More of the sounds and feelings, more of Mack's balls slapping against his ass.

"More," Justin said in a guttural tone that felt like it was pulled up from his gut. "More!"

"I'll give you more," Mack promised him. He hitched Justin's legs up beside his ears. "Better hold on."

Justin had to let go of his dick to grab the backs of his knees, but he did it. Mack rewarded him by fucking him so hard he was pushed up the bed.

Mack braced a hand above Justin's shoulder, helping to keep him in place. He pounded into Justin, and

Justin had a flash of clarity—he was going to come, and come hard, and all without a hand to his dick.

Justin bellowed when his climax hit him, rolling up from inside his ass to his balls and on out his cock. His vision blurred before erupting into a thousand bright white dots. He felt raw and open, as if Mack could see into his soul as cum spurted from his slit.

Mack grunted with every hard thrust into him. His rhythm disappeared and he fucked Justin like a wild thing mating in a frenzy. It was all Justin could do to keep from screaming out his joy at being taken so completely.

Everything in him was satiated when Mack rammed into him and froze. He could feel the heat inside him as Mack filled the condom with cum.

Mack's garbled yell had a triumphant ring to it, and he ground against Justin one last time before gasping. Justin let go of his legs and grabbed for Mack, pulling him down on top of him.

After several minutes, Mack muttered, "Condom." He reached down between them then pulled his cock free. Justin couldn't keep from moaning in protest, even though his ass was already stinging.

"Damn, Jus," Mack said as he flopped down beside Justin. Justin turned his head and got a sloppy, sexy kiss from Mack. "Can I see?" Mack asked when it ended.

Justin frowned, wondering what the hell he'd missed. "See what?"

Mack's entire face turned dark with a blush, but he wiggled down some. "Here," he explained.

Justin jolted when he felt Mack's fingers on his ass. Mack slid them over to touch his hole. Now it was Justin's turn to be embarrassed. "Why?"

Mack shrugged. "Never mind."

Justin hadn't intended to make his lover feel bad. He shoved aside his reticence and cocked his leg. "No, it's fine. I've got nothing I want to hide from you."

Mack looked at him then he traced that tender skin again. "Feels hot and puffy. I was just worried, because I was so rough."

"Oh." Justin didn't know what to say to that. It'd been a long, long time since he'd had anyone worry about him. Some of the other Marines in his troop, maybe, but only in a team sort of way. It wasn't personal, so much, not really.

"It's okay?"

"Yeah," he assured Mack, although he was confused as to whether Mack meant to look, or how his ass felt.

Mack manoeuvred him onto his side and started scooting down again. Justin guessed that meant he'd agreed to the first. Mack parted his butt cheeks, pushing the top one up. It made Justin's poor hole ache and he didn't quite manage to stop a hiss at the pain.

"You're sore," Mack said.

Before Justin could answer, Mack was kissing him there tenderly. "I'm sorry," he said between light brushes of his lips.

"It's fine. Weren't you sore?" Justin asked, wondering if he'd be able to handle another fucking. It'd be worth it, he decided, especially if he got this sweet treatment afterwards. The only problem was he could hardly keep his eyes open. Mack had fucked him out to the point of exhaustion.

"I was, but not too bad," Mack told him. "I think I was rougher on you."

"You were perfect," Justin replied. "Now come up here and let me hold you before I pass out."

Mack chuckled and placed one last kiss on his pucker. "All right then. I could use a nap myself. Let me get a wash cloth and wipe up the mess you made when you came." He winked at Justin, a teasing smile on his face.

Justin tried to keep his eyes open, but it wasn't happening. He squeaked when he felt the cool, wet rasp of cloth over his dick. He hadn't realised Mack had been gone long enough to get the cloth. Mack wiped him down, then the bed dipped and Mack was right there beside him.

It was perfect, and what he'd longed for ever since he'd taken off. Justin twined his fingers with Mack's, then he let sleep carry him away.

Chapter Ten

It wasn't yet morning when Justin woke up with Mack plastered against his back. He'd come back after going to the JMR to handle some business Craig had said couldn't wait. He'd been right, as it'd been a delivery of cattle he wasn't expecting yet. Justin was still leery about messing with the critters, but Craig and the other hands assured him they had it under control. Justin would have been fine with just raising good Quarter horses and Thoroughbreds, but that would have been too much direct competition with Mack. Cattle seemed like a compromise, he thought.

Mack had been dozing off when Justin'd returned, so there'd been nothing more than a few kisses between them before they'd both fallen asleep. Ranch life and sex with Mack, combined with the emotional turmoil of the past few days, had worn Justin out like nothing else ever had. The Marines had sent him some places that had tested his physical endurance to the limit, and he had his share of scars, more psychological than not, from some of the things he'd seen and done. But none of those had turned him inside out like talking about the past to Mack had done. And seeing Mack, first so full of hurt and hate, then the sympathy in those beautiful blue eyes—well, it wrenched Justin inside.

The outside, however, was getting jabbed at by a stiff cock. Justin cracked one eyelid open and saw nothing but darkness and a blurry green light. Alarm clock, he realised as Mack rocked his hips against Justin's ass.

Justin was a bit tender in the backside, but his cock was waking up and ready for playing. He rolled over and draped an arm around Mack's shoulder. Blinking, he tried to see through the darkness to discern if Mack was awake. There was a wet gleam that he took to be Mack's eyes. Seemed to be in the right place.

"Eh, cowboy, think you can spare a hand?" he asked, keeping a straight face though he supposed it didn't make a difference considering the lack of light.

Mack snickered and poked him in the belly, and not with his rigid dick, either. Justin squealed and slapped at Mack's hand. "Cut it out, Mack," he said breathlessly as Mack kept on tickling him.

"Aw now, that was about the corniest line I've ever heard," Mack told him. "I think it earned you some punishment."

Before Justin knew what was happening, he was guffawing and wrestling on the bed with Mack. There was a pang of familiarity doing it, reminding Justin of when they'd been boys, innocent and tussling about like they'd tended to do.

Then Mack was kissing him, and Justin didn't feel anything but alive and horny. Mack fisted their cocks and stroked a couple of times. "Do mine," he rasped, and Justin nudged Mack's hand aside enough to get a hold of Mack's shaft. The long, hot length was lined with thick veins, and Justin contemplated getting his mouth on that perfect cock.

But Mack began jerking him off, and Justin responded instinctively, working Mack's length in return. "Love the way you feel in my hand," he mumbled, searching out Mack's lips in the darkness. "In my mouth—" He licked Mack's lips, delved his tongue in when they parted for him. "In my ass." Except maybe not for a while. He needed a day or so to recover. "In my heart," he whispered so quietly he didn't think Mack heard him.

Mack twisted his wrist around, rubbing Justin's cockhead in a way that had him panting for breath. "You like that, bub? Feels good, I bet."

Justin did the same thing to Mack and was glad to hear Mack's soft moan. "Does, don't it? Ung." Mack teased the bundle of nerves on the underside of Justin's crown. "God, Mack, you're gonna kill me." It'd be a fucking fantastic way to go, though.

"Uh-uh, you can't blame me if you bite it. You're the one who asked for the hand," Mack pointed out. He stopped long enough to lick his palm then resumed jerking Justin off. Justin didn't have a chance against that wet glide on his dick. He hissed and fucked Mack's hand, stabbing hard into that grip.

"Gonna come, baby," he got out right before Mack hummed his approval. Spunk shot from his cock and Justin felt his eyes roll back in his head as he grunted.

"So fucking sexy," Mack crooned, working the cum right out of him. "You make the best sounds, Jus."

Justin made a few more sounds, rocking into Mack's hand until he couldn't stand to be touched, his cock too sensitive for it. Then he shook himself, remembering what he was supposed to be doing.

Justin took a move from Mack's playbook and licked his hand, coating his palm liberally with spit. He closed it around Mack's length and at the same time, craned his neck so that he could kiss Mack.

Without warning, he set a hard, fast rhythm that he matched with thrusts of his tongue. Mack grabbed onto him, nails marking Justin's skin, leaving stinging trails behind them as he worked Mack's cock.

Within a minute or two, Mack threw his head back and groaned. He jerked hard against Justin then came in hot spurts between them. Justin wished he could have seen it, but he settled for bringing his hand up and licking the cum off his fingers.

"Are you..." Mack leant forward and Justin felt a tongue on the back of his hand. "You are." Mack made a contented sound and licked some more.

Justin's cock was threatening to come back to life, but he had to get back to the JMR, at least for a few hours. He didn't think any of Mack's hands knew he'd stayed over—Craig had followed him on horseback and more or less dropped Justin off last night. Minx would have been noticed if Justin had tethered her outside, or put her in a barn or pasture.

"Craig should be coming back with Minx..." Justin flopped over and looked at the alarm clock. It was a little after four in the morning. "Shit. In about twenty minutes. I gotta get up and meet him."

Mack shuffled around on the bed, and Justin shivered when Mack traced the path of his spine with a fingertip. "You could stay. I don't owe anyone an explanation."

"No, you don't, but I already told Craig to bring Minx at four-thirty, so I can't leave him hanging. He'll already be on trail as it is." More than likely, Craig was already at the appointed meeting spot. "I don't want to out you to everyone. That's something only you should do, and we didn't discuss it before we fell asleep last night."

"I know." Mack sighed and rested his head on Justin's shoulder. "You're right. Go on, and I'll deal with having to shower by myself."

"That's playing dirty," Justin said, but he twisted around and kissed Mack's lips. "But I do got to go. I'll be back later today, if that's okay with you."

"It is."

Justin imagined Mack had more questions, and while that made Justin feel a tad nauseous, he would do whatever was necessary to ensure they'd have a life together.

His phone buzzed and Justin huffed as he got up. "Fuckin' Craig's probably texting me to hurry up." He walked to the dresser, visualising the room to keep from walking into anything. His cell phone was still lit up, too, which helped somewhat. "Yep. 'Hurry up, boss, or I'll be drinking your coffee'. Asshole," he muttered even as he smiled.

"He makes me nervous," Mack said with enough reluctance in his voice that Justin turned to him.

"Why? I told you we weren't messing around, that we never had. You can ask him, too, if you want." Justin didn't want to have to fire Craig, but if it was him or Mack, there was no question about who he was choosing. He could find another foreman, although not one he trusted like he did his Marine buddy.

"It's not that. He just seems, I don't know, dangerous, I guess," Mack confessed. "God, that makes me sound like a wuss or something."

"No, it makes you sound like a smart, observant man," Justin corrected. "Craig can be meaner than a rattlesnake and way more deadly. Rattlers don't always have control, and they don't always mean to kill when they attack. Craig, well, he pretty much does both. I'm not saying he's a killer as in the murdering kind, but he's done what he had to for his country. Many times."

"That's... I don't know what to say to that." The bed springs squeaked and footsteps sounded on the floor. "Be careful, okay? And...and come back."

Justin winced, knowing he'd not given Mack a reason to believe he'd hang around despite the words they'd exchanged. He had years' worth of abandonment to get Mack past.

"I'll be back, I promise. If I'm not back quick enough to suit you, you know where I live." Justin hugged Mack, needing to feel him in his arms one more time before he had to go. "You're welcome at the JMR any time."

"Okay." Mack embraced him and they stood for a minute, just holding each other.

Justin's phone buzzed again. "I better get dressed and head out."

Mack snorted and let him go. "Yeah, you don't got enough hair to be doing that Lady Godiva bit."

"Don't have the right parts for it, either, as it happens." Justin reluctantly moved away from Mack. He used the flashlight app on his phone to find his clothes. Last night he'd just left them where he'd kicked them off.

"Let me hold your phone while you get your stuff together. You can get dressed in here or in the bathroom."

Justin handed Mack the phone. "I'll get dressed in the bathroom then hit the road. Try to get a bit more sleep. I plan on wearing that ass of yours out later."

"Jesus," Mack hissed. "How is it you can make me hard again so fucking quick?"

"Same goes," Justin said. He leaned in for a kiss then took the phone back in the hand that wasn't holding everything he'd shucked the night before. "I'll be back."

In the bathroom, he washed the spunk off his belly and groin with a washcloth then rinsed the rag and left it on the side of the tub. Wet towels and cloths in the hamper led to mouldy everything in there, especially in the humidity. He dressed quickly and quietly left the house. Mack hadn't spoken when Justin had checked on him. He hoped the man would get some sleep.

Justin only had a short walk to where Craig was waiting—which wasn't where they were supposed to meet. That was farther back, into the scrub and mesquite, well past the house and barns, but Craig was only a couple dozen yards away from the back door.

Justin didn't bother scolding Craig. He'd probably said in the second text where he'd be. Justin hadn't bothered to read it. After he mounted Minx, they rode out back towards the JMR. Craig waited five long, hellish minutes before speaking.

"Got your coffee here," he said as he reined his horse to stop. He held out a metal thermos.

"Were you waiting for me to beg?" Justin asked, taking the container from Craig. "That was the longest five minutes of my life," he teased.

"Right," Craig scoffed. "Any of the times we were pinned down by snipers passed in the blink of an eye, but having to wait for coffee was interminable."

"I try not to think about those times," Justin admitted. "Only thing that kept me from losing my shit on more than one occasion was the thought of Mack."

"That's sweet. Drink your coffee before you share any more shit like that."

Justin didn't take offence at Craig's gruff order. He knew the big man was teasing him.

The coffee was hot and strong, and Justin figured he scorched a path down to his belly as he drank it eagerly. The caffeine would hit his bloodstream soon and he'd be ready to get started on his day.

"So, is this going to be a regular thing, you sneaking around to see Mack?" Craig asked, looking off towards where the sun was beginning to break through the sky.

Justin couldn't be sure if that was insulting or not, then he decided it wasn't an untruth, exactly. "I didn't want to out him, I told you that last night."

"Yeah, you did." Craig turned back to face him. "But what I want to know is, is he going to treat you like a dirty secret? Would he do something like that for payback?"

Justin's temper spiked and he didn't care if Craig was bigger, badder, deadlier. He walked Minx up to Craig's mount's side. "Mack's a more honourable man than that. But if he wanted to treat me like shit, I'd let him. Whatever he needs to feel better. Whatever it takes to convince him to take me back, that I won't leave him again. And whatever that is, it isn't your business."

Justin didn't wait for an answer. He turned Minx and gave her her head, letting her take him home.

* * * *

Mack walked out to the corral with his third cup of coffee in his hand. He was feeling groggy, but the caffeine had to kick in eventually. He hoped. Taking a sip, he looked at the red stallion glaring back at him and figured he'd better come up with a good routine to gentle this beast.

His own father had been brutal at times, once even taking a bat to a horse after it'd kicked at him. Mack had been sick, literally puking when his father had done that. He'd only been a kid, maybe six or seven, and terrified of his old man. He'd had good reason—when he'd begged his father not to hit the horse, he'd threatened to take his anger out on Mack's hide with that bat. Sometimes Mack still hated himself for not taking a stand. He got that he'd been a kid, but it always seemed like he should have taken a stand regardless.

Mack didn't believe in abusing an animal any more than he believed in abusing a kid. It wouldn't happen on his ranch. He started running options through his head.

There were more methods for taming a horse than he could recall—that whole horse-whispering phase had brought every horse trainer in the world out of the wood work to write a book on the best way to tame a horse. Mack preferred a gentle hand, a kind voice and lots of patience. A few sugar cubes, carrots and apples helped, too.

None of which he'd brought with him. Mack turned, thinking he'd get some goodies out of the barn, and nearly ran over Leo. The foreman was short and on the scrawny side. Those were the words Leo used to describe himself, but age was showing in the paunch on his belly and the deep lines framing his mouth and eyes. Mack didn't quite suppress a startled sound that escaped him when he turned and saw Leo. He hadn't even heard the man approach.

Leo grinned at him until his eyes lit on the love mark Justin had left on his neck at some point yesterday. Mack wasn't even sure when he'd done it, but there was no hiding the lurid purple mark. He saw the moment it hit his foreman just what that mark was and who had likely put it there.

"Goddamn it, Mack, what the hell are you doing? Didn't you learn nothing twelve years ago?" Leo all but shouted, glaring like he'd slap the shit out of Justin if he thought he could get away with it. He was shaking with anger, and his hands were fisted at his sides.

Mack wondered what the hell was going on with his foreman. This didn't look like friendly concern. This was blatant hatred, something he'd only seen a time or two before on Leo's face. Leo's scowl deepened and he took a step forward, as if trying to intimidate Mack.

That wasn't going to happen. Mack's temper began to rise as Leo moved even closer. Mack refused to back up. He levelled a furious look at Leo. "What the hell's your problem?"

Leo cursed and Mack gripped his coffee mug so hard he was surprised it didn't break. He took a deep breath, the memory of his father's temper cooling his own. Mack wouldn't be like his old man, not for anything. He wanted to knock the shit out of Leo, to push him back and get the foreman out of his face, but Mack refrained from doing so. He was the boss here.

"Drop it, Leo. It's none of your business," he growled. Mack moved to walk around him, but Leo stuck out his arm and grabbed Mack's wrist, pulling him to a stop.

"You made it my business when you told me what happened between you and Justin years ago, so don't get all pissy with me," Leo snapped back. "You came crying like a little girl and I listened then, so you can fucking listen now."

That was it, Mack had had it with pig-headed assholes. The coffee cup shattered in his hand, and Mack felt it slice into his skin, which only incensed him even more. He dropped the remains of the mug and grabbed Leo's wrist hard enough that he felt he man's bones rubbing together. Mack squeezed a little harder, the pressure making the pain of his cut worse, which in turn made his anger bubble over like a pot of water left too long on the stove.

"I have purely had it with people grabbing me, Leo, do you hear me?" he snarled, taking perverse pleasure in the fear he saw leap into the other man's eyes. A small voice chided him, warning Mack he was going to end up like his father if he didn't watch himself. Still, Leo's continued belligerence, the 'fuck you' he saw forming on Leo's lips, eclipsed his reserve.

"What I told you twelve years ago does *not* give you any right to interfere in my life, and it for damn sure doesn't give you any rights over me. I was a dumb, scared kid when I came to you, and believe me when I tell you I fucking regret that now. And get this through your head," he said, leaning closer until he was right in Leo's face. "I will fire your ass if you ever cross that line again, understand me?"

"Is there a problem here?"

Mack tipped his head up enough to see Justin striding across the yard to the corral.

Mack put his attention back on Leo. "I dunno, Leo. Is there a problem here?" He almost prayed the man would say yes. Mack didn't want to deal with any more bullshit from Leo.

Leo jerked his wrist out of the blood-slicked grasp Mack had on it. He turned and stormed off without answering either of them.

"What the fuck?" Justin said, almost shouting it. "What happened to your hand?" The look of rage on Justin's face was intense and immediate. It doused Mack's anger in an instant. He stepped in front of Justin when he would have gone after Leo. "Move, Mack. I'm going to kill that stupid fucker."

Mack slapped both hands against Justin's chest. He grabbed Justin's shirt and dug his boot heels into the ground for leverage so he could use his body weight to prevent Justin from going after Leo.

"No, you aren't, because I'd be purely pissed off if I have to find another foreman," Mack said. "Not unless you're gonna give me yours." His attempt at humour fell flat. *All righty then,* he thought. It wasn't like he wanted Craig working for him anyway.

Mack decided to try reasoning with his stubborn red devil. "Justin, come on. He didn't hurt me. I broke the coffee mug and cut myself." That seemed to get through a bit, because Justin quit trying to get past him, but he didn't look any less furious.

"Just what exactly was going on when I walked out here then?" Justin asked, cocking his head in a way that conveyed agitation. "What the hell did Leo do that made you angry enough to let loose on him? Don't bullshit me, either, because I have never seen you so mad. You might feel some sort of...of loyalty for that man, but he don't deserve it."

Justin grimaced and went on. "And I sure as shit don't owe him anything other than a serious lesson in manners. I know he provoked you first, cowboy. You aren't the kind to start trouble."

Justin glared at him, narrowing those brown eyes as if he thought that would prevent Mack from disputing his claim. There was no reason for Mack to, despite that look. He actually had to bite back a grin, because he wasn't stupid enough to think he could get away with lying to his lover. Not that he'd have done so in the first place.

Mack took a long breath, trying to think how best to word the whole situation. He'd always been direct and wasn't fixing to change that now—but he could put some more distance between Justin and his foreman first.

"Look, let's go inside so I can clean up my hand first. I need to see how much I screwed it up by being stupid, okay? I think it's just a shallow cut, but I haven't looked close, so let me fix it up then I'll tell you what you want to know." Mack watched his lover and slowly eased his grip when the anger in Justin's expression was replaced with one of concern.

"Shit, I'm a jerk." Justin swiped his hands over his face then looked at Mack's hand. "Let's get you taken care of first. Then you can tell me what happened. I promise to hold off beating the tar out of that idiot until then." The teasing curl of his lips and the sparkle of Justin's eyes took the heat out of the threat.

Justin took Mack's injured hand gently and cradled it in his bigger hand. He didn't seem to be concerned with anyone else seeing them, and Mack decided he didn't care either. He wasn't going to hide who he was with from anyone, he'd wanted Justin too long to do that, and this was a start to letting those around him know he was done hiding.

They walked across the yard and up the porch before Justin held the porch door open. Mack went inside and headed straight for the kitchen. He hadn't looked too closely at his hand yet.

"Where's your first-aid kit?" Justin asked.

"Bathroom cabinet." Mack walked to the kitchen sink to rinse his hand.

"All right, you stay right there. Don't move. I'll help you rinse it off when I get back with the kit." Justin darted out of the kitchen.

Mack waited by the sink, kind of flustered by the attention. He was a grown man, after all, and hadn't had anyone to fuss over him in ages. He'd been sick and hurt before with no one seeming to care as long as they got paid on time. He wasn't sure he was going to like being cosseted. Grumbling, he told himself he was a man, not some clingy kid. He turned on the water and stuck his hand under it.

"Ow ow owowowowow! Shit! Ow!" Maybe he was a clingy kid on the inside, because that hurt like a motherfucker. *Buck up*, he told himself, then he glanced at his hand and saw the gash that ran down his palm from right above the pad of his thumb. "Uh." Why was his head trying to spin around? Or was that the room?

"Goddamn it, Mack! I told you not to move!" Justin raced across the kitchen, carrying the first-aid kit. Watching Justin move so fast made Mack feel even dizzier, and queasy to boot. Justin slipped one arm around Mack's waist then looped Mack's arm over his shoulder.

"You look a little green, and shaky, too. I don't like you shaking unless it's when you're under me or over me or beside me... Well, you get the picture. Now lean on the counter here and let me see that hand." Justin took Mack's injured hand before Mack could find the coordination to raise it up. That angry expression slid over Justin's face again.

Mack looked down at his hurt hand and felt his stomach lurch. Jesus, he was such a wimp! He could handle injuries on animals and other people, but his own blood and torn flesh was disgusting and sickening. A rumbling laugh drew his attention back to Justin.

"I could be wrong here, but maybe you should stop looking at the cut? I can clean up your hand, but I'm not so good with emptied-out stomach contents." Justin even blanched when he said it.

"Yeah, that's probably not a bad idea. Wouldn't do for both of us to be laid out on the floor...hmmm. Then again, maybe—" A pinch to his ass had Mack yelping, jerking his mind right out of the gutter. He glared at Justin. "What'd you do that for?"

Justin rolled his eyes, a visual 'duh'. "Had to get your mind off that particular horny track before I forgot about your hand and spread you out like a feast on the floor. I'd make you my own personal picnic."

"Mmm," Mack mused. "So if I told you that really turned me on, what then? Would you make me forget everything else but the way you feel inside of me?"

Justin's groan was tinged with a healthy dose of frustration. "What, me spreading you out, the pinch, fucking you on the floor—which of those were you talking about?"

"All of them," Mack admitted, because it was easier than confessing how much he'd liked that little bite of pain from being pinched. But Justin looked at him shrewdly, then smiled seductively.

"How about I promise to pinch your ass the next time I'm fucking you? I bet you'd like that."

God, that promise sucked the breath right out of Mack's lungs, but he still found the strength to nod, even as he blushed.

"All right then, count on me bringing up a patch of pink on your fine ass." Justin's voice had grown deeper with need. Mack's cock responded by pulsing uncomfortably against his zipper as Justin talked. "Sit down at the table then I want to look at your hand again."

Justin led him back to the table and pulled out a chair for him. Mack sat and held his hand up, trying not to look at it. Instead he watched as Justin set the first-aid kit on the table and opened it up. He pulled out tubes and gauze and various other things. Mack managed a wobbly smile when Justin glanced at him. That was the best it was going to get when he felt like his stomach was trying to turn inside out. Justin leaned in and gave him a soft, chaste kiss.

"I don't think it needs stitches, but maybe we should have a doctor check it out after I put some antibiotic ointment on it, just to be safe."

Mack shook his head. "No way. I saw the... I saw it enough to know it'll heal up without stitching. It ain't that bad, just long's all." *And gross. That's my skin sliced open.* Mack swallowed back bile. "Nope, I don't want to go to the doctor. You just do what you need to do then wrap it up."

Justin stared at him for a second then nodded. He took Mack's hand and turned it. Mack averted his gaze and tried not to think about what Justin was doing. The flooring in the kitchen needed a good sanding down, he decided, then a fresh layer of sealant over it. Probably the whole house needed the floors re-done, but that would take time and energy Mack didn't have to spare. Having someone else do it would mean being inconvenienced in his own home, so that wasn't happening.

"Now, tell me what happened with Leo," Justin said, interrupting Mack's thoughts in a deceptively silky voice.

Mack knew Justin was struggling to keep his temper in check again, and he appreciated the attempt. He just hoped Justin could manage to do it. "All right, but you need to understand something." He turned his head back to face Justin.

Justin cracked his knuckles then pressed his hands against his thighs, fingers spread wide. "I'll try, but right now I just want to beat the shit out of him, Mack."

Mack huffed but wasn't mad. He knew he'd be feeling every bit as mean if he were in Justin's boots. Justin growled and Mack arched an eyebrow at him. "You going to listen, or are you going to sit there and do your best rabid dog imitation?"

Justin arched a brow right back at him and scowled. "Start talking. Please."

Mack was glad Justin had at least added that last word, because he was wavering from one emotion to the next. He didn't want to have this conversation, didn't want to delve into the past again. Justin deserved an explanation, though. He steeled himself against the memories that tended to make him hurt more than any cut on his hand ever could.

"After...after you left, I was fucked up, Jus. Angry, hurt" — *broken* — "whatever you want to call it." Mack paused upon seeing guilt wash over Justin's features. "Look, Justin, I'm not telling you this to make you feel bad, okay? I'm just trying to explain why Leo was acting like a fool, maybe. I'm not really sure what his problem was, but this is all I got." He waited until Justin nodded to continue.

"Okay then. Leo had always been a little more than an acquaintance, not quite what I'd thought of as a friend, back then. He was older than me, and I guess maybe I just didn't have no one else after you left." Mack hitched up his shoulders in a shrug. "He asked me what was wrong when he found me in the barn, sobbing like a baby denied the tit, you know. I didn't know what to tell him when he asked me what was wrong. I tried to get him to leave me be. I was humiliated as all get-out, him seeing me like that."

Mack really had thought he'd die of shame in his teenage melodramatic way. He paused, weighing the effect his words were having, not wanting to cut Justin now for something that happened back then. When he was sure Justin was holding up okay, he continued, but he reached over and held Justin's hand as he did so.

"Eventually, I gave up on making Leo go away, and I told him what happened. I figured..." Mack's vision went hazy then, memories coming to life in his mind. "I figured if he freaked out over me being gay, then he'd freak and either try to beat the shit out of me or whatever. I surely couldn't feel any worse than I did at that point." He shook his head and gave Justin an apologetic glance. "It feels like everything I'm saying is an accusation instead of a simple accounting. That's not my intention. I just don't know how else to tell it."

Justin stared him straight in the eye and Mack would swear he could feel the sorry rolling off the man. "It's all right, Mack. I know I hurt you. I'll regret that until the day I die, and longer, even, if such a thing is possible. I always figured my hell would be knowing you never forgave me, but it might be knowing how much pain I caused you regardless of whether or not you forgive me."

Mack opened his mouth to speak, but Justin held up a finger, gesturing that he wasn't done yet. Mack closed his mouth and listened.

"It doesn't matter that leaving wasn't what I wanted, or that it tore me up to do it. I'd spent so long thinking about the future I wanted for us, that I had hoped to share with you back then, and it was all taken from me, from us. When you get down to it, even the why of it doesn't matter. The truth may make the pain dull and fade, but it can't unwind a dozen years or heartache and betrayal. It can't soothe the pain then, or all the years in between, for either of us."

Mack leant forward and touched Justin's arm, hoping to comfort them both. "No, nothing can take that pain away, true enough, but maybe I—we—can find some way to get past it, yeah?" Leaning back when Justin nodded, Mack resumed his story, trying to watch his words and yet be honest.

"So, Leo knew what happened, and he saw me go through that, tried in his own way I guess to help me. He didn't condemn me for being gay, exactly, but he did preach at me. I thought it was his way of showing his concern for me." Mack sighed. "I just didn't have anyone else, so all I could do was either keep everything locked inside of me, or talk to him. I talked. When I told him what I said to you, before you left, he got really agitated." Mack shook his head as Justin glared.

"I didn't understand that. It took me years to realise he might feel something for me that was, uh, wrong in his mind." Mack frowned. "It was wrong in mine, too, with him. Trust me when I tell you the feeling was never reciprocated. I felt bad for him, though, and while I never had any proof I was right, I still think maybe I was, especially after today. The thing is..." Mack's voice ground out on him and he cleared his throat.

Justin knelt in front of him and tenderly stroked his cheek. "Tell me," Justin pleaded softly.

Mack had to clear his throat a second time, but he finally found his voice. "I felt even worse knowing that I wouldn't change it, none of it. Not your friendship, not what we did, not the pain when you left, not the vows I made you —" He almost stopped at that, remembered his guileless promises to Justin made with all the enthusiasm and earnestness of youth. "Telling you that I would always love you, and always wait for you. Because I do, and I have, Justin. All these years, I've loved you and waited on you."

God, he felt like his chest was going to burst right open, and he couldn't seem to stop the tears from spilling down his cheeks.

And Justin...his beautiful brown eyes were glimmering with moisture that flooded out as well. Justin shifted on the floor then he pulled Mack out of his seat and down onto his lap. He held Mack as if he were the only good thing left in the world.

"Mack, don't you know that I love you more than life, more than my next breath? I don't even have words." He paused, staring at Mack with a ferocity that shook him to the core. "There are just no words that can describe it, but you should know that I never forgot your vows. Believing in them, believing in you — the dream that one day, I'd be able to come back and be with you again." Justin sniffled and pressed his forehead to Mack's. "Those were the only things that kept me going, that kept me sane. Without them, I wouldn't have bothered trying to survive my tours."

Mack felt something inside him break off and rush up to his mouth in a hot wave. How could Justin profess to love him so much, yet walk away rather than stay and fight for him? Justin would rather take on the insurgents intent on killing him than to try to salvage a chance for them? *What. The. Fuck!*

Chapter Eleven

He saw the anger rip through Mack, pulling his mouth into a thin line. Justin braced himself for a lashing, and Mack didn't disappoint.

He pulled back but didn't rise up from Justin's lap as he asked, "Then why, Justin, why didn't you stay? Why didn't you fight for me like you fought for your country?" Mack demanded of him. Justin didn't even get a second to answer before Mack barrelled on.

"Because if you had loved me back then like you say you did — do — you would have stayed. We could have taken on your dad or anyone else who gave us shit. We could have run off together. You don't love someone like that and just walk off after telling them 'thanks for satisfying my curiosity'!" Mack yelled, chest heaving with the force of his emotions.

Justin shook him gently, afraid Mack was in another time and place in his head. He needed Mack to listen, to hear him. Justin pulled Mack close and caressed his back with long sweeps of his hands.

"I told you that my father found out. I didn't finish the rest of what I was trying to tell you about that, but

Bailey Bradford

now..." Justin tipped Mack's chin up and stared at
him. "Now you are going to let me finish, and you're
going to listen, okay?" He waited until he could see
Mack pull in some of the pain he was feeling, getting
himself under control. That was his cowboy, so strong
and resilient. Justin was grateful every fucking day
that Mack wasn't the type to give up easily.

"All right." Justin thought back to the other day then
nodded to himself. "I told you that son of a bitch
pulled me through the door. It was bad." Which was
an understatement. Justin still didn't know how he'd
survived that beating. Mack had gone pale, his tanned
skin almost ghostly white.

"I can see you get the idea, but it was worse than
you think, I can promise you. I know at eighteen, most
people would wonder why I didn't fight back, and
maybe I should have, finally, except...except after the
first punch, he told me—" Justin stopped, his heart
aching like he was in danger of it giving out on him.

"What'd he tell you?" Mack asked quietly. "Tell me,
Jus. I need to know."

Yeah, he knew Mack did. Justin closed his eyes for a
moment. "I can still hear him, Mack, in my head like
he's standing in my skull hollering at me. Like he's
pulling me back in time." Justin snapped his eyes
open, hoping to escape that hellish voice. "He told me
he would kill you for making me a queer. He'd put a
bullet right here." Justin kissed Mack between the
eyes. "I couldn't let him hurt you, Mack. I couldn't
risk it. I'd have done anything to make sure you were
safe."

Mack sobbed but quickly sealed his lips together
until he seemed to be calmer. His eyes were red-
rimmed from tears, and his hands were gentle on
Justin wherever he touched. "It's okay, Jus. You don't

have to go on. I understand. I couldn't have risked you, either."

It wasn't forgiveness, exactly, but it was close, Justin thought. He needed more than that to ease his soul. "I do have to go on. I have to tell you. Maybe it will get us both past what I did, and let us start over new."

Mack tilted his head in a way that Justin knew meant he was considering Justin's words before replying. "All right, but just remember — it's done, it's the past. What's most important is right now, this very moment, and each moment we create together. I didn't realise it, I was too busy being pissed and hurt, but it's true. None of the bad things matter anymore, as long as I have you."

Justin tightened his arms around Mack and leaned into him. "I love you, Mack. So much. Let me just get this out, just finish it so it's never between us again." Justin dragged air in his lungs and rested his chin on Mack's shoulder. "He said he'd kill you for making me a faggot, because no son of his was going to be gay. He'd beat it out of me if he had to. Then he proceeded to try his best, telling me all the while how as sheriff, he could kill you and get away with it. I've never been so scared, Mack. I couldn't let him hurt you."

"So you said, and I get it, Justin, I do." Mack turned his head and nuzzled Justin's neck. It felt so good, so loving, that Justin's eyes burned again with unshed tears. "Get it all out and let it go. The past can't hurt us anymore."

"You're right, of course you're right," Justin murmured, turning his head to find Mack's lips. The kiss was brief, but it chased the chill of the past out of Justin. He sat up and looked at Mack. "So. So I told him I wasn't gay after the seventh or eighth punch, I don't remember. Dad was so careful to keep the hits to my ribs and back or my legs." He always had been, except once or twice when Justin had had to use the old 'fell down the porch stairs' excuse. "I would have told him I was anything he wanted me to be if it kept him away from you. I said I was just curious because I found one of his magazines he kept hidden."

Justin snorted at that. "He thought he had them where I'd never find them, but a teenage boy and porn aren't to be parted. He'd confiscate them from people, I guess. Maybe he bought them, I don't know. But they weren't all straight porn mags, let me tell you. He was definitely an angry, repressed man."

"Sounds like," Mack agreed, surprise evident as he spoke. "Wow. I never would have guess. So, did you tell him gay sex sucked?"

Justin almost smiled at that. "Yeah, I did. Figured if I couldn't do it, he sure wasn't going to be thinking about trying it and enjoying it. I'm sorry to say I told him plenty of lies about it being bad." Justin was relieved to see Mack smile crookedly at him.

"As long as you were lying," Mack hedged.

Justin nodded. "Oh, you know it. I couldn't really say what it felt like to have sex with a girl, but he didn't need details, just me spouting off about how much tighter a pussy was than, you know, anal sex. I wasn't going to let him know there was nothing so fine as pushing into the heat of your ass, of feeling you inside, bare on my dick."

"We were probably stupid for not using condoms back then," Mack mumbled, his cheeks ruddy.

"We were both virgins," Justin pointed out. "We admitted as much to each other."

Mack conceded the point without further argument, going back to the confrontation between Justin and his father. "I know you didn't mean it, but I can see that you had to tell him what you told him. Your father would probably have beaten you to death if you hadn't."

"I was so afraid he'd come after you," Justin admitted, then he spoke of another fear. "I was afraid he'd want to try—that he'd rape you and kill you afterwards. I feared he'd do that to other men, anyways. He wasn't right." In fact, Justin often thought his father had been evil through and through.

Mack was gaping at him like he'd blown Mack's mind.

"What?" Justin asked, "You don't think he was dangerous?"

Mack shuddered and swallowed before answering. "No, I do. I do, and I just thought about how he could have…done…that. I'm so fucking glad he didn't. I'd rather he just have killed me than had him in me."

"I'd rather he just be dead," Justin admitted. "It's awful of me, maybe, but I wanted him to die for so long. I couldn't have hated anyone more than I did him. He made me twist something I cherished so much, and turn it into a lie for survival. But as long as it meant your survival, I accepted it. I'd have done anything, would still do anything, to anyone, however I had to do it, to protect you."

Mack peppered his face with kisses, speaking in between each one. "I know how you feel. I would do the same. I don't blame you anymore, so please, don't blame yourself. If it's forgiveness you need from me, you have it. You have everything I have, everything I am." Mack sat back and frowned as Justin's pulse raced with something very much like euphoria at Mack's words.

"I have to tell you, Jus. If your father wasn't already dead, I might seriously have killed him myself if I'd known." Mack frowned harder. "Maybe I'm a bit off upstairs."

Justin chuckled and brushed Mack's hair off his brow. "No, I don't think so. He was a bad, bad man. I hated him for as long as I remember. I guess, maybe, at some point, I wanted my daddy to love me—but I can't remember it." No, because his father had been a vile, hateful, abusive fucker. "The day I walked back and met you at the pond, the first time, the only time we made love before I left, my father was up on the ridge, watching us. I guess he had his suspicions. He was there again the next day, when I was on more pain meds than a mule just so I could walk. I knew he was holding his rifle, and he was just waiting for me to fail to convince him that I meant what I'd told him, that I just was using you."

Justin remembered seeing the glint of the sun off the rifle barrel. "I was so fucking scared that I was going to be talking to you one second, then see a bullet hole—" He couldn't finish that and shook his head.

"It's okay now," Mack told him right before cradling Justin's face in his hands. The gauze was rough on Justin's skin, but he could feel the heat of Mack's palms and it warmed him to his soul.

"I need you," Justin whispered, feeling the words in his core. "I've always needed you, cowboy. I always will."

* * * *

Mack felt something inside him lighten and shift free, pushing out all the pain and anger he'd carried around for so long. He felt light without that burden, as if he could float up into the air, but he had no intention of getting that far away from Justin.

"You've got me, always," he said before standing up, keeping a hold of Justin to bring him up at the same time. Mack kissed him, suckling on his lips, pushing at his tongue and making them both moan with need before he backed off. "Come with me." He hooked an arm through Justin's and they walked to the bedroom.

They stopped in the room and the wonder and need he saw in Justin's eyes was another balm to his soul. They reached for each other at the same time, with Mack bringing up his injured hand to cup Justin's face. God, he hadn't thought it was possible to love this man more, but it was, and he did. The emotion was almost overpowering.

Justin closed his eyes at the caress and tipped his head forward, meeting Mack for a slow, lingering kiss. He slid his hands down Mack's arms then began working the buttons free on Mack's shirt.

Mack couldn't get enough, caressing Justin's cheeks, his throat, his shoulders. Justin paused to pet and touch him often, sharpening the edge of Mack's desire until his cock was as hard as it could be. Justin pushed his shirt off and Mack scrambled to get Justin's off as well.

When Mack reached the button on Justin's jeans, he opened it but rather than going for the zipper, he slid his hand down to cup the hot bulge of Justin's cock.

"Yes," Justin said through gritted teeth. He pinched Mack's nipples and Mack gasped. Justin's smile was pure wickedness. "I haven't forgotten what else I get to pinch up into a pretty shade of red."

Mack clenched his ass cheeks as anticipation warred with nerves. "If I don't like it…"

"I'll stop," Justin promised, then he leaned in and whispered in Mack's ear. "But you'll love it." He pinched Mack's butt through the layers of jeans and underwear, but the sting came through and Mack moaned, his balls pulling up as he thrust against Justin.

Justin unzipped Mack's pants and began pushing them down. "Uh-uh, don't want this ending before it really begins."

Mack groaned but quit trying to rub off on his red-haired devil. "Fine, but you better hurry up and get naked, bub." Justin licked his lips, then he licked Mack's. "Mmm." Damn, Justin tasted good.

Justin pulled back and guided Mack to the bed. "Sit, and let me get the rest of your clothes off."

"Like I'm going to say no to that," Mack told him, plopping onto the bed and bouncing a bit. "Boots?" He held up his left leg.

"Guess that'd be the smart way," Justin agreed before tugging the boot off. "Next."

Mack lifted his right leg. When Justin grabbed his boot, Mack leant back on the bed and propped himself up on his elbows. Justin tossed the boot near the other one. He peeled off Mack's socks then turned to tug off his jeans and underwear. Mack squirmed around, trying to help him, and they had him naked in seconds. Justin stood up straight, breathing heavily as he looked Mack over, and Mack finally understood what it meant to be visually devoured.

"Damn, you're just fucking beautiful," Justin muttered. Beautiful was something Mack had never been called, and he would have scoffed at the word had it been anyone other than Justin who called him such. Justin darted a glance to Mack's dick. "Stroke yourself while I strip for you. I want to watch, but don't come."

Mack nodded, already reaching for his shaft with his good hand. It wasn't the one he usually beat off with, so his strokes were a bit jerky, and he was in no danger of coming from them. Now, the look in Justin's eyes? That was something that could make Mack spurt like a damned geyser if he wasn't careful. He watched Justin pull off his boots and socks, rubbing his thumb over his leaking slit to spread around the moisture gathered there. He trembled, an almost violent contracting of his muscles as his nipples began to tingle. Mack risked a little pain, bringing his injured hand up to scrape over one taut nub.

"Oh," he sighed, surprised at how good it felt to touch his own nipple. He hadn't messed with them before. If Justin hadn't showed him how sensitive they were, he'd have missed out on this. Mack lowered his eyes, watching Justin pushing and shoving to get his jeans down. He figured that meant Justin was turned on by Mack's show.

Mack pinched at his nipples and just worked the head of his cock. He spread his legs, then bent them and brought his heels to his ass, offering Justin everything.

Justin crawled onto the bed, right on up Mack's body. He braced his knees against Mack's butt, pushing Mack's heels aside, and he hooked one hand under Mack's arm. With a heave, Justin shoved Mack up the bed, centring him on the mattress.

"I won't ever get enough of you," Justin said right before he plundered Mack's mouth, filling him with Justin's slick tongue and addictive flavour.

Mack held onto Justin's biceps, feeling small quivers under his hands as he met Justin stroke for stroke. His lips felt bruised and swollen by the time Justin raised his head. There was a question in Justin's eyes that Mack didn't quite get.

"I swear to you, I'm clean. I didn't come all this way and wait all this time to put you at risk."

Mack nodded. He knew military members were tested for every damn thing under the sun.

Justin's Adam's apple bobbed and he glanced away before focusing on Mack again. "And you, uh. You said...you said you waited for me." Justin's gulp was audible. "Do you mean you haven't—not since—"

Mack was uncomfortable as hell, but this was the man he loved. There'd be no lying. "I meant it, Justin. I couldn't. Not with anyone else. I had made those vows, and there wasn't anyone to tempt me, even. I just...I just worked here, on the ranch."

God, he hoped that was enough. Justin stroked his hand down until it encircled Mack's engorged dick. "Can we—do we have to use the condoms?"

If it were anyone else but Justin—Mack stopped the ridiculous thought. It'd never been anyone but Justin, never would be, either. "Yeah, I mean, no, we can ditch them."

Justin's smile was bright enough to melt the coldest heart, and Mack's certainly wasn't that. "Thank you," Justin said. "I don't ever anything between us again."

"Me either." That was easy to agree to.

Justin gave his dick a squeeze, much to Mack's delight. "So," Justin drawled. Something about the way he said it had Mack blushing from the top of his head to the bottoms of his feet. Justin's grin was triumphant. "That means there are toys here, somewhere. Besides the sheep."

The images that shot into Mack's head had him groaning. Just the thought of using some of his toys on

Justin... "Oh fuck, Jus. I want to fuck you with this big dildo I have — later. Right now, I need you, not a toy."

"You've got me, cowboy." Justin bent and bit Mack's nipple.

"Jesus!" Mack tried to sit up, tried to grab Justin's head and press him down to his chest again. "Don't stop!"

"Wasn't going to." Justin kept a hand on Mack's dick while he went to work sucking marks up on Mack's pecs. He teethed each nipple until it felt hot and sore, and Mack wanted to scream for more *something* to make him come.

Justin left off torturing his nipples in that pleasurable way and lapped a path down to Mack's cock. He sucked the crown right into the warm cavern of his mouth, and Mack shouted like a man who'd found gold.

Mack thrust up, unfettered by Justin's hands. His cock sank deep into Justin's throat, those slick muscles contracting around his tip.

"Oh, oh fuck, Jus...Justin," he panted.

Justin came off his shaft and licked right up to Mack's belly button, where he proceeded to delve into the shallow well there.

Mack was going crazy with arousal, unable to keep still. He shifted his legs on the bed, he wasn't satisfied with his hands on any one spot on Justin because he wanted to touch that sexy man everywhere at once. Mack wanted to wrap around him like a second skin.

Justin dived down on his cock again and Mack keened, dots dancing before his eyes as his pulse shot into warp speed. He was aware of Justin pushing something into his mouth beside Mack's cock, but it didn't register what until Justin pushed two spit-slicked fingers into his ass.

Mack went off like a tea kettle reaching full boil. His keening ratcheted up higher and his ass clamped down as cum jetted from his cock. Justin flicked his tongue over Mack's tip, drinking down his spunk. Mack ripped at the sheets, uncaring of the pain spiralling up from his injured hand.

Before he could recover, Justin was rolling him over. Mack had barely landed on his stomach when Justin parted his ass cheeks and began eating his ass.

"Jus!" Mack arched his lower back, trying to spread his butt more, to get Justin's tongue inside that pucker. "Fuck me!"

Justin pinched him then, a hard, sharp bite of pain that flared bright and raced from Mack's buttock up his spine and around to his nipples. "Again, oh sweet Jesus, do it again!"

Justin teethed his hole at the same time he delivered another pinch, almost right in the same spot as the first. Mack's cock tried to perk back up. If Justin did that a few more times, he'd be hard as a diamond again.

Justin not only did it a few more times, he pushed his fingers into Mack's ass, right beside his tongue. Mack like to lost his head when Justin stroked over his prostate and pinched his ass cheek hard enough it had to raise a welt.

"Please, Jus, please," Mack was moaning, rocking his head from side to side as he tried to get his knees under him. Justin kneaded his buttock with hard, gripping presses of his hands. Mack's cock was erect and he was desperate to have Justin fuck him, but articulating that wasn't possible when he kept gasping and groaning.

Justin pushed his butt cheeks so far apart it made Mack's hole ache. Then he pressed his face into Mack's crease and licked deeper into him than he ever had.

"Justin!" Mack barked out, shoving back eagerly. "Fuck me already!" He shouted it loud, but Mack was beyond caring who heard. He needed Justin badly.

Justin swatted him on his butt once, then did it again and again. Mack met him with a backwards thrust for every one of those hits.

Then Justin was on him, putting Mack on his side. He shoved Mack's top leg up, and cold, wet lube was poured over Mack's hole. He yelped indignantly, but Justin pushed two or three fingers into him, warming him in ways that made him want to melt.

"Raise this leg up more," Justin said, tapping Mack's raised one. Mack caught it with his arm, hooking the back of his knee with his elbow. "Beautiful, baby."

There was that word, beautiful again. Mack liked it, a lot. Justin pumped his fingers in and out of Mack's hole a few times, then he straddled Mack's leg that was straight on the mattress. He grabbed Mack's butt again, pulling the top cheek up. Justin's crown was right there at Mack's pucker, teasing him mercilessly. Justin leaned over him and grabbed Mack's shoulder.

"Love you, Mack," Justin said right before thrusting and burying his cock hilt deep in Mack.

"Ah, yeah," Mack whispered. "Move, Jus, move."

Justin did—no gentle start to this fucking. He pounded into Mack relentlessly, repeatedly, grunting with every slam of his hips against Mack's backside.

Mack got a hand on his dick and began stroking himself off, need coiling hot and tight inside his groin. Justin lowered himself down and his dick rubbed over Mack's gland with every thrust thereafter.

"Yes, gonna come," he panted out when Justin began hammering him with short, deep movements. Mack sped up his hand-to-dick contact, then he was babbling he didn't know what as he came.

Justin gripped him tighter and fucked him harder. Wet heat spilled into Mack's ass when Justin grunted again and froze, his cock as deep inside Mack as it could get. Feeling Justin's cum spurting into him pulled Mack out of his post-orgasmic haze. He knew he was wide-eyed and gawping, but man, that felt weird and sexy and it'd probably be a bit gross when he stood up. It was definitely something he wanted to do again, often.

And filling Justin up with his cum? *Yeah, I wanna do that. Fuck him and come in that tight ass as many times as I can in a day. Have him stay flat on his back in bed, or get one of those plugs I've read about…*

Justin shook like a nervous Chihuahua then he carefully laid down behind Mack, his cock still inside Mack's hole.

"I know I can't stay here forever," Justin said huskily as he rocked his hips. "But man, if I could, that'd be awesome."

Mack clenched his butt, giving that cock a good squeeze. Justin yelped and grabbed at Mack. Mack peered over his shoulder at Justin. "I came twice, how about you? Think you can get it up again?"

Justin's slow smile was all the answer Mack needed.

Chapter Twelve

Craig looked at him as Justin rode into the yard. Justin wouldn't have come back to the ranch at all that day, but he did actually have some work to do.

Craig's slow grin as he looked Justin over was kind of unsettling. "Looks like someone's been rode hard and put up wet. Or is that, someone's been riding hard and putting someone else up wet?"

Justin flipped the ogre off. "You're just jealous 'cause you only have your hand for company."

Craig smirked at him. "Says who? You think there's only us three gay men here or in town?"

Justin was *not* slack-jawed. He snapped his mouth shut. "You're lying."

Craig shook his head. "You really haven't paid attention to any other man in town, have you? Because some of them surely don't try to be subtle."

Justin shrugged. "Why would I? There's always only been one man I wanted."

"I don't understand that," Craig admitted. "Don't mean I don't respect it, but I just can't see myself ever being tied down like that."

Justin dismounted and smirked right back at Craig. "Well, see, there's part of your problem. It isn't as awful as you're making it sound. I sure wouldn't call it tied down, not like a prisoner or a dog on a rope."

Craig looked as sceptical as a man possibly could. Justin shrugged. "There's no use trying to explain it when you don't want to hear about it."

Craig glanced away. "I saw the way my parents fought, and it wasn't any different when they divorced and remarried other people. It was always drama and screaming and cheating, all of them. I don't imagine I'd be any different, and don't see a reason to risk ruining anyone else's life." He faced Justin again. "The vet's with the new cattle in the east pasture."

Justin mounted back up. Craig got on his big ol' mare, Firebrand. She wasn't quite as red as the hellacious stallion back at Mack's, but she was gorgeous. Maybe he'd see about breeding the two of them together.

"You've never mentioned anything personal before," Justin pointed out as they rode to the east pasture. He'd thought about not bringing it up, but hey, Craig had started it.

Craig grunted and cut him an irritated look. Justin wasn't scared. He glared back. "Get over it. If you didn't want to talk about it, you would have kept your mouth shut. You are not a chatty guy."

Craig bared his teeth and Justin laughed. So did Craig. "Fine, fine. I don't really want to talk about it, though. Guess I just had a freak moment of being the sensitive type. It won't happen for another decade or four."

Justin snickered and didn't doubt it.

"So what happened at the cute boyfriend's place today?" Craig asked. "Besides sex. You smell like sex, Justin, you know that?" Craig shifted in his saddle and glared at Justin again. "I don't care that I don't want to fuck you, or your boyfriend, but goddamn, smelling sex makes any man horny."

"Good thing you know all the available pieces of ass around then," Justin quipped.

"Fuck you," Craig grumbled. "I said there were other guys, yeah, but I don't like cheaters. The one guy I know who *is* interested and isn't partnered up with someone else isn't my type. Maybe I could make an exception, though."

Justin barely kept from rolling his eyes. "By all means, do the guy a huge favour and fuck him. I'm sure that'll make his life complete and he can die a happy man."

"Yup, that's true. I've got the magic dick."

Justin choked on his retort and had to try again. "You *are* a dick, Craig. I almost think you're serious."

Craig looked at him and didn't crack a smile when he said, "Why do you think I'm not?"

Justin shook his head. "With an ego like that, you'll be alone forever." Or have all of the twink ass he could find.

Craig confirmed that with another smirk. "Nah, I have guys throwing ass at me when I go out to the clubs looking for it. I have to duck to keep from getting hurt, it's flying around so fast."

"All except for the guy who isn't your type," Justin couldn't resist pointing out. He frowned at a horrible thought. "That really isn't me, or Mack, right? Or Leo?"

Craig laughed so loud and long Justin was tempted to thump him upside the head. He swiped at his eyes and snickered again when he glanced at Justin. "Leo, the ugly little shit that's your boyfriend's foreman?"

"My boyfriend's name is Mack," Justin corrected. "You know that."

"I do, but he's also your boyfriend, and that's cute in a fussy, girly kind of way."

"Fuck off," Justin said tiredly. "You're not so amusing anymore."

Craig shrugged. "Wasn't trying to be, so that's okay. And no, it isn't any of y'all, but especially not that little creep. Now that we've picked and bitched at each other, you want to tell me what happened at Mack's place? You can go into detail about the sex if you like. Maybe I could give you pointers."

"What the hell got into you today?" Justin asked, but it occurred to him that he probably had his answer in something Craig had said earlier. The guy who wasn't his type. Justin would bet that was so because he'd turned Craig down flat. Craig obviously felt he had something to prove, and was doing it by being an ass. "Never mind." He'd rather not try to make Craig admit it.

"So, sex?" Craig asked.

Justin clucked his tongue and got Minx to step it up a bit. "Nope, not going there with you, but you sure nailed it when you called Leo a creep." Justin filled Craig in on what had happened earlier. Craig looked fit to tear the man apart.

"You do realise he wants what you're getting?" Craig asked.

"Yeah, we figured as much. Ain't going to happen though." Not when Mack hadn't been with anyone besides Justin, ever. "I worry about Mack, though. I don't think Leo has all his oars in the water, you know. He might even be paddling with a couple of cane poles."

Craig chuckled at that and Justin didn't really have anything else to say. They rode in silence until they were only a few minutes from their destination.

"He might cause trouble," Craig said then, echoing thoughts Justin had been mulling over. "Can you talk Mack into firing him?"

"That isn't my place," Justin said without having to consider it. "Besides, firing him might push Leo over an edge we don't want him falling from. You know the saying about keeping your enemies closer."

"Yes, that way they can stab you with a shorter knife," Craig quipped.

Justin was uneasy the rest of the day. He would be staying with Mack every night from now on, if Mack would let him.

* * * *

Mack walked over to the barn, figuring that was his best shot of finding Leo. Leo hadn't answered his cell or Mack's call out to him on the radio handset. That was a big no-no on the ranch. Leo was the foreman and should always be reachable unless he was actually on his own time away from the ranch.

He'd given Leo a couple of days to cool off, but more than once he'd spotted Leo glaring and muttering when Justin was in the vicinity. Mack had had enough of it. This was his property, his home, and Justin was his man.

Hopefully Leo would be rearranging tack or doing inventory of the supplies in the barn. No one else was around, the other ranch hands working out with the horses, moving them to different pastures. Mack

Bailey Bradford

would rather not have anyone overhearing what might be said. This was going to be a private conversation between him and Leo.

Mack wanted to try to prevent any kind of scene that might prove to be humiliating for Leo, at least around witnesses, because an audience could bring the ass out in anyone, even a normally rational man—which Mack was beginning to think Leo wasn't.

Still, they needed to work out this issue of Leo hating Justin. Preferably peacefully, because Mack wasn't ever doing without Justin again. Leo needed to accept it. If he'd ever been any kind of friend to Mack, he *would* accept it, because he'd want what was best for Mack and that was definitely Justin.

And surely if Leo knew the truth about what had happened to Mack and Justin, if he knew why Justin had said those hateful words and left, he'd forgive Justin, eventually. Mack had the moment he heard Justin's telling of the events. He knew the truth, and he knew the man he'd loved for so long.

However, if Leo didn't back off about Justin, well, then all bets were off. Leo's ass would be gone before sunset. If he insulted Justin, Leo would be lucky if all he got was fired. Mack was feeling fiercely protective of the lover he'd only just found again. Or, more correctly, who'd found him again.

Opening the door to the barn, Mack noticed the hinges didn't squeak any more. That was good. He liked knowing the place was being maintained properly when he didn't always have the time to repair things himself. He'd spent the last couple of days replacing boards in the loft and on his back porch, along with helping to build another corral. They'd need it, with the JMR's horses due to arrive next week.

154

Mack checked the barn and the tack room, but Leo wasn't anywhere around. He guessed he could check the bunk house, though it damned sure better be empty. No one had claimed to be sick or anything.

Mack closed the door as he stepped outside, his eyes watering as he went from the darker lighting of the barn to the bright as hellfire sunlight. He spotted Leo striding up to the main house, looking puffed up like he was just full of righteous indignation. That, or he'd got a stick wedged up his ass.

Either way, Mack thought this would work. They could have this discussion in the privacy of his own house. It'd probably be much better than a possible screaming match in the barn, where there were pitchforks and other sharp objects. Plus, they wouldn't spook the horses. He quickened his step and reached the stairs just as Leo started pounding the hell out of the door.

"Been looking for you," Mack said from behind Leo, causing the shorter man to jump and yell. Leo faced him, and Mack knew this conversation would be going down hard. There was too much anger in Leo. Mack could practically feel it pulsing off his foreman. *Better get this inside ASAP.*

Keeping a calmer façade than he felt, Mack nodded to Leo. "Looks like you got something on your mind, too. Save it until we're inside." He opened the door and gestured for Leo to precede him. Leo made a beeline for the living room, but Mack stopped him with a short, "No. Not in there."

Leo spun around and gave him a hateful look. "You want to do this in here?"

Mack lifted his Stetson up and ran his fingers through his hair. "Do *what* here, Leo? What exactly are you planning? An intervention of some sort?" Mack shook his head when Leo only continued to glare at him. "Go to the office. You know where it is."

The office was the best place for the coming confrontation. Mack should have spoken to Leo sooner about his outburst the other day. Letting him stew for a couple of days had obviously only given Leo more time to build up his reserves of anger. If Leo had another outburst today, Mack didn't think he could hold back, and he sure as hell didn't want to end up trying to toss Leo through his nice big-screen TV in the living room.

Leo turned on his heel and headed past the living room, kitchen and into the hall. His boot heels struck the floor hard enough to leave scuffs, which Mack suspected the asshole was doing on purpose. Leo had been in the house plenty of times, going back to when Mack's dad had run the place.

Leo took a left, entering the office across from Mack's bedroom. He stood sullen and belligerent-looking, reminding Mack of a badly aged teenage kid with no manners.

Mack strolled over to his desk and sat in his comfortable, beat-up chair. It occurred to him that he could simply fire Leo flat-out for his attitude, but that didn't sit right with him. He had to try to be as fair as possible before resorting to yanking a man's job out from under him.

Mack was tired of the drama swirling around Leo, and he told himself to be calm, rational, all the things a boss should be. His damned mouth never seemed to listen to him when his brain said shit like that. "You want to tell me what the hell you thought you were doing with that little tantrum you threw the other day, and all the days since, skulking around and glaring fit to kill?"

As badly as Mack wanted to cringe and smack himself for his outburst, he forced himself to keep still and not let his gaze waver. He hadn't yelled, or raised his voice at all. He just hadn't been as calm as he'd meant to be.

Leo jutted his jaw out, which sent his jowls to flopping in a disturbing way. Mack glared back at him, determined not to blink first. Leo finally looked away, staring at some point to Mack's right, probably out of the window. Mack could almost see the thoughts racing around in Leo's head. Did the man not expect Mack to be pissed off, too?

Maybe, Mack thought. After all, he'd not really stood up to Leo about anything over the years. There hadn't been any reason. All their possible issues had been about work, and hiring or firing people, along with the occasional sermon Leo tried to pitch him. Mack had always zoned out when he'd done that.

So Leo probably hadn't expected Mack to take a stand. Well, that was too bad. Mack just hadn't had anything worth fighting for before. Leo could try to find a way to work this in his favour, but Mack could have told him it wouldn't happen. An icy calmness settled over him as he watched Leo patiently.

Once Leo seemed to have come up with a plan, he looked at Mack again. Leo loosened his jaw, appearing to Mack like he was trying to wipe his true feelings off his pugnacious features.

"Look, Mack, I was worried the other day. I still am. How could I not be, considering that you're hanging around that bastard?"

Mack wasn't buying Leo's concern, or at least not his reason for it. There was too much anger and disgust in his voice, and something Mack instinctively distrusted in his eyes. Leo had always known Mack was gay.

While he said he didn't condone it, he hadn't ever gone so damned batshit crazy on Mack.

Which told him this was all about Justin, unless Leo was one of those who believed Mack could be gay as long as he didn't act on it. Mack didn't think that was the case, though. He slowly shook his head. "I don't think so, Leo. Something about your whole manner doesn't ring true to me, and regardless of what you may feel, you do not have the right to manhandle me. Ever. Period. Grabbing me outside the other day was reason enough for me to fire you. Do you understand me?" Mack leant back in his chair and propped his elbows on the desk so he could steeple his fingers as he considered Leo.

"Maybe I need to make something very clear to you. I'm your boss, and as such, there are lines you never cross with me. We've never been the best of friends, but I counted you as one." *Sort of.* Mack locked his fingers together to keep from pointing, something that would only spark more anger in Leo. "I'd think a friend wouldn't be trying to make me miserable by being an asshole to my lover."

Leo flushed so dark his face was almost purple as he sputtered. "Fine!" Leo yelled, spit flying as he did so. "I'll tell you what the fuck I thought I was doing." He approached the desk and slapped his hands down onto the top of it. "I was trying to keep you from making the same sick mistake you made a dozen years ago!"

Knowing Leo thought he wasn't going to Heaven because he was gay was something Mack had had to deal with a few times. Hearing Leo spew such venomous words was altogether more difficult to deal with. It was like being slapped with a prickly pear, making Mack sting all over from the insult of it. He also thought he must have been wrong about Leo having a closet crush on him. The way Leo had said the word 'sick' was nothing short of the sick itself.

"And what, exactly, do you mean when you refer to my 'sick mistake', Leo?" Mack said with a calmness he no longer felt. He'd be damned if he'd show that now.

Leo's eyes seemed to bug out of his head with the force of his fury, his face going darker still and red blood vessels becoming prominent in the whites of his eyes. "What do you mean, what sick mistake? You know what I mean. I mean letting that dirty queer touch you again! How could you!" Leo shouted.

Mack had to scoot his chair back to avoid the splatter. He stood and the second Leo was done screeching, Mack whipped an arm out and grabbed the front of Leo's shirt. He jerked and had Leo halfway over the desk. Mack felt mean and dangerous, not trusting himself just then not to physically hurt Leo.

"If I were you, foreman, I would be very, very careful about what words you use and how you use them. Do you understand me? Maybe I didn't speak up before Justin came back, because frankly, I didn't have the desire to touch any other man, but that never meant I was anything different than I am—gay. So I suggest you stop flinging slurs around, because I am purely fed up with your insane behaviour. Don't push me anymore. In fact—" Mack released Leo and backed up. "In fact, I think you're done here. I don't have to put up with you talking like that about me, or Justin, or anyone. I don't allow the men to use any other slurs, and you aren't any exception to that rule."

"No," Leo said, stumbling back a step. He tripped and landed on his butt. Just as quick, he got up and ran around the desk to confront Mack. "No, I know you aren't one of them, Mack. I know you aren't. Twelve years and you never fucked another guy! Everyone knows qu—gays are promiscuous. They can't help but fuck each other, don't matter if they are lesbians or like Justin. You ain't like them, I've watched over you for more'n twelve years, making sure. Don't let one stupid mistake you made when you was a kid drag you back down!"

Mack was astounded by the illogical everything in that speech. "What the hell do you think me and Justin have been doing, playing dominoes every night and morning in my bedroom?" He could have added 'at lunch, too', but that would be rubbing it in Leo's face. "Jesus, man. You don't even realise that you sound like a raving lunatic, do you? You need some help, Leo." Shaking his head, Mack started to turn away. "You need to pack your shit and go, too. I'll give you a month's severance as well as your retirement account."

He got one step before Leo grabbed him by the shoulder. Mack spun around, throwing a punch before he even thought about it. It connected with Leo's jaw, sending a shockwave of pain up Mack's arm from his knuckles all the way to his shoulder.

Leo went tumbling backwards, arms flailing and his feet going out from under him. He hit the wall and slid down it. Mack thought he'd knocked him out until Leo cupped his jaw and stared at Mack like he'd never seen him before.

Mack reckoned Leo had never seen him fight back. There'd never been a cause for him to. Mack had sure stunned himself as much as he had Leo just then.

He backed away, getting behind his desk again before he ended up doing something else he'd regret—though he wasn't sure he regretted decking

Leo at all. Maybe just that it had hurt his damn hand to do so.

"Something you should know, Leo? You thought you were keeping me chaste?" Like that wasn't embarrassing, and Mack had been too blind to see it. "You thought you were keeping me from being gay, that you saved me from some horrible fate?" Mack couldn't hold back a laugh at that nonsensical way of thinking. "The truth was, Leo, that you thought you were saving me, when all this time, I was saving myself—for Justin. You had *nothing* to do with me not fucking around. It was all Justin, and the love I feel for him. I don't give a shit what you say, there isn't anything wrong with that kind of love."

For a minute, he thought Leo might actually speak, but Leo finally grunted. *Whatever that means.*

"Now, I'm telling you for the last time, Leo. Pack your gear and leave. And so help me God, if you use the word 'queer' or any other slur on my ranch again, I'll make it so you can't speak until the doctor can unwire your jaw once it's healed." Mack meant it, too, even if he did sort of not like the fact that he'd do it. "I am gay, I'm telling you again. I've always been gay, always will be. I have gay porn, and gay toys—"

Leo held up a hand, but Mack just kept talking.

"I thought you understood that. You didn't 'save' me, or whatever screwed up idea you have in our head. I never needed saving. Seems to me you should be more worried about your own self with all the hate you're carrying around."

Leo narrowed his eyes until Mack couldn't even see the colour of the irises. "But you're not a faggot, Mack. You're not one of them."

The futility of the conversation, if it could be called one, finally hit Mack. Leo was never going to get it.

Either he couldn't, or wouldn't. It didn't matter which. Movement in his peripheral vision caught his attention, and Mack turned to see Justin standing in the door way, hands white-knuckling the frame. How long had he been standing there? Long enough if the expression on his face was any clue.

"You!" Leo exclaimed. Mack and Justin both looked at him. Leo stood up, using the wall to brace himself as he never stopped glaring at Justin. "This is your fault, perverting Mack all over again." He took a step forward. Mack came around the desk, whether to put a stop to Leo's tirade or to keep the man from Justin, he wasn't sure.

But Justin shook his head. Something in his eyes made Mack stop and move back out of the way. He trusted his lover's judgement. It couldn't be worse than his own, which had his hand throbbing even now.

Leo was so worked up he was practically frothing as he shouted. "I saw you perverting Mack years ago, you sick son of a bitch. I saw you trick him, and put your—" Leo's lips peeled back in a look of disgust. "You fucked him. I don't know what you gave him to make him go along with it, but now he thinks he's like you and even worse, he thinks he loves you! Like that's even possible! Your father should have fucking killed you when I told him what you did!"

Mack was so shocked, he forgot to breathe.

Justin, however, let out a roar that had every hair on Mack's body standing up in alarm. With a ferocity that had Mack sucking air back into his lungs, Justin sprang from the doorway and lunged at Leo, who met him halfway. Leo threw a jab at Justin's belly, but he was no match for the bigger man. Justin grabbed his arm and spun him around before slamming him face-first against the wall. Justin pressed a hand to his neck and shook Leo like a dog with its favourite fetch toy. Then Justin watched with an almost detached manner as Leo struggled for air he wasn't able to get.

"Do you have any idea what you've done, Leo? Any idea how much pain you caused to a man who thought you were his friend?" Justin's voice was as devoid of emotion as his expression. "Any idea what you nearly cost us? Of the toll your sick mind exacted on us? We lost twelve years we could have been together, you fuck. All because you got jealous. You watched me and Mack and couldn't stand that you weren't man enough to have him. I bet you're hard right now, you perverted scumbag."

Mack found his coordination then and ran over to pull the two men apart. He was seriously afraid his red-haired devil's temper was completely out of control. While he still felt the urge to beat Leo himself, Mack didn't want the man dead. Not really, and certainly not by Justin's hands.

"Justin. Justin, stop," Mack said in what he hoped was a loud, firm voice.

Justin didn't even bat an eyelash. Leo was turning an ugly shade of dark purple, and in a near panic, Mack reached under Justin's armpits, trying to get his own hands underneath the one strangling the life out Leo, the damned fool.

Before he could pry Justin off, Justin let go on his own and caught Mack's hands in his. Leo slid down the wall and landed in a puddle on the floor. He was conscious, though, but he looked like pure shit.

Justin tugged on Mack's wrists, pulling him up flush to his chest. He kissed Mack, then turned him around so his back was to Justin. Justin folded their arms over

Mack's belly and began to rock them from side to side in a gentle movement.

Mack stroked soothing circles over Justin's arms as best he could, trying to chase away the anger he was sure still skittered around under Justin's skin. They both glanced down at the man who'd caused them so much grief with his hatred, and, if Justin was correct, his jealousy.

Justin pulled his arms free and gave Mack's belly a pat. He stepped around Mack then and bent to grab Leo by his arms. Justin jerked him to his feet and pushed him back against the wall. Mack was ready to intervene if necessary, but Leo only leaned against the wall and Justin let go of him as soon as Leo did so. Leo wobbled almost immediately and Justin slapped a hand to his chest, none too gently. Leo opened his mouth to say something Mack was sure would be vile—and stupid, he couldn't forget stupid—but Justin didn't give Leo a chance to speak.

"Don't say a word. Not. One. Word, or I'll finish what I started, you understand?" Justin didn't wait for a response. "Mack has asked you to gather your things and leave. He wants you off his ranch. He asked— now I'm *telling* you to do it. And you better understand something." Justin paused, the silence emphasising the seriousness of his words that followed. "If you ever, ever set foot on this property, near this property and definitely anywhere near Mack again, I will tear you apart, and no one will ever find the pieces when I'm done with you. Got it?"

Jesus, that about scared Mack—and gave him wood. *That's just a bit messed up, maybe. Oh well. Works for us.* Looking at Leo, he saw that Justin had pretty much got the point across to the man, as all of the colour had leached out of his face, and… Mack sniffed. Okay, maybe it wasn't the shit that Justin had scared out of Leo. Mack leaned around Justin and saw that yes, Leo had indeed pissed himself.

"That's gross, man." It seemed an apt assessment to Mack.

Justin glanced down and saw the same thing Mack did on Leo's pants—a big, growing urine stain. Mack smiled like a cold, evil bastard, he hoped, and he slowly took a step back.

"Looks like you understand me," Justin said. When Leo nodded jerkily, Justin finally removed his hand, freeing Leo to leave.

"Get gone, now," Justin told him. Somehow it was more deadly-sounding spoken softly like that than if Justin had shouted it.

Leo bolted from the room like a cat with something stuck to its tail. He bounced off the door frame in his haste to escape then he was gone, nothing more than the sounds of his retreating footsteps and the smell of piss to remind them he'd been in the office.

Mack winced and fisted his hand. He had that to remind him, too. Justin turned him and hugged him suddenly, tightly.

"Damn, Mack, he was here the whole time. I thought my father had seen us, but it was him. It was him who went and told my old man, who—"

"Yeah, he was here," Mack said, cutting Justin off. He wanted to wipe away the worry and regret Justin was carrying around. "But he's gone now, and he didn't hurt me. He didn't. I did, however, hurt myself when I punched him."

Justin pulled back and looked at his hand. "The same one, Mack? Did the cut even get to heal?"

"Well no wonder it hurts so much." Mack held his hand up and saw blood. "Ugh."

"There's not a lot, just seepage, I think."

"That's fucking nasty, man." Mack didn't want to look at it for fear he'd puke. "And the office smells like piss."

"Yeah, it does, and I can clean your hand up for you again. Come on." Justin kissed him, and Mack parted his lips. Justin slid his tongue inside, twining it with Mack's in the most delicious way. Mack even forgot about his hand, about the mess Leo had made. Justin drove it all from his mind as he brought Mack to full, throbbing hardness.

"Hand first," Justin informed him a minute or two later. It could have been half an hour, for all Mack knew. He'd been lost in that kiss and the way Justin felt pressed against him.

"Fine," Mack grumbled, because his hand seemed to suddenly have a million and one screaming nerve endings letting him know it fucking hurt.

Justin kissed him on the tip of the nose—Mack wasn't sure what to think of that—then he held Mack's sore hand gently and headed for the bathroom. The first-aid kit had been put back up after the other day, so Mack could understand why Justin chose the bathroom. Why Justin turned on the shower when they hadn't really worked up much of a sweat yet was another thing entirely.

"What are you doing?" Mack asked when Justin got the knobs adjusted how he wanted them.

"All I can smell is that asshole's piss. I think he stared wetting himself when I was spinning him around or something." Justin wrinkled his nose like he was really smelling something rank. Mack didn't sniff to see if he was right. He wasn't stupid.

"Okay." Mack started to undress, but Justin moved over to him and took his hand.

"Let me take care of rinsing this first." He turned Mack's hand palm down. "You scraped your knuckles on the dumbass' face, too. Come over to the sink."

Mack let Justin take care of him because it felt good this time. Both of them had been on edge, and Justin had maybe got closer to it than Mack had. Or maybe not. He was beginning to think Justin never had lost control back in the office.

After his hand was cleaned off and properly kissed according to Justin, Mack was slowly stripped of his boots and clothes. His hat had come off somewhere in the office—hopefully nowhere wet. Justin undressed after he had Mack nude and in the shower, then he joined Mack under the spray.

Chapter Thirteen

There'd been a few minutes when Justin had been running down the hall to the office that he'd been scared for Mack's life. Justin thought about that as he soaped Mack's sexy body up.

After Justin and Craig's talk about Leo, he'd been inclined to think Leo was well past unstable and into raving lunatic range. Hearing Leo's raised voice had caused a spike in fear that had probably given him a few grey hairs, not that he was going to look for them.

Then to find Mack, so strong and determined, looking like a hardass fucker who'd snap Leo in half — Justin had stood in the doorway and watched, awed by his lover. Mack was just amazing, there were no other words to describe the way he'd handled Leo. If Justin hadn't showed up, Mack would have got rid of Leo eventually.

But Justin had taken a small measure of enjoyment in confronting Leo. It wasn't the physicality of it that he liked. Being a bully had never appealed and he damned well felt like one pinning Leo to the wall like he had. Unfortunately, that seemed to be the only thing Leo understood, brute force.

It had been finding out the truth, though it had burned like a hot poker to the gut. Still, Justin had been able to confront someone. He'd never stood up to his dad, having stayed away from the bastard until he was dead and buried. Only then had Justin visited him in his grave. That had been more to make sure his old man was really in there than anything else. The tombstone said he was. That was good enough for Justin.

"Where are you at, bub?"

Justin snapped back to what he was doing—which was, apparently, soaping the same spot on Mack's chest repeatedly. "Sorry, I was just thinking about everything. It's a lot, you know. All this time I thought it was my old man who'd seen us, but it was a different Peeping Tom."

Mack scrunched up his mouth like he'd eaten something rotten. "Don't remind me. I think I'd rather it have been your father than someone I worked with every damned day for over a decade." He swiped water off away from his eyes. "Do you really think Leo was jealous? Because if he was, why didn't he ever try anything? Not that I wanted him to," he added quickly. "I'm just trying to understand it. Him."

Justin went back to paying attention to where he was cleaning, enjoying the feel of Mack's wet, slick skin beneath his hands. "Well, I don't think there's any understanding him. And yeah, I think he was jealous. He wanted you, but he had that whole bullshit bigot thing going on. Like my dad." Justin stopped, a horrible thought occurring to him. "I wonder—"

"God, don't," Mack said, turning in his arms. "That's just too disgusting to even contemplate." He looked through his wet lashes at Justin. "And I have better things for you to do, like fuck me, then turn around and let me pound away at this bubble butt of yours." Mack stroked over his butt, dragging his fingers right over Justin's asshole.

"Uh." Justin wiggled a little, hoping to get a bit more action back there.

"I don't think so, stud. Me first." Mack pushed the shower nozzle aside and handed Justin a bottle. It was too big to be lube. He looked down and saw that it was conditioner. Justin took it and opened the cap.

"All that snarling and rough stuff you did turned me on, you know," Mack told him as Justin poured out some of the creamy stuff. "I guess I shouldn't be surprised, considering how much I like it when you pinch my ass and my tits, right?"

"Turned me on when I heard you, and when I saw you deck Leo, my dick almost busted through my jeans, I got hard so fast." It hadn't held, because he'd been angry and scared, too, but for a minute there, he'd considering jumping Mack right in front of Leo.

"I'm not going to punch you," Mack told him, winking or blinking water out of his eyes. "Unless you keep stalling. Then I might have to."

"Can't have that," Justin murmured. He ran his conditioner-coated fingers over Mack's hole. That tight little ring quivered for him and Justin pushed two fingers in just enough to ensure Mack felt it.

"Oh, more, please," Mack said, pushing back eagerly.

Justin could still see the bruises from where he'd pinched Mack in some places. As much as Mack had enjoyed it, Justin would be doing it again, soon. Wet skin, however, was not conducive to pinching. There was no way to get a good grip. Justin settled for slapping Mack's ass several times as he fingered his hole. That pinked up that pale, pretty skin real quick.

"I don't wanna come yet, I don't wanna come yet," Mack started chanting when Justin inserted a third finger into his hole.

"I don't want you to come yet, either. You're supposed to fuck me next." It was fun to drive Mack into near-babbling, though.

"If you keep stimulating my prostate like you're doing, I'm gonna be decorating the shower walls in a minute."

Justin pulled his fingers out, ran them over his cock to coat it with some of the conditioner. Without any more teasing, he grabbed Mack's hips and pushed into his tight channel.

"Aw, yes. Fuck me, Jus." Mack dropped his head down against the tiles.

Like Justin needed telling twice. Mindful that they were in the shower, the tub floor wet and slippery, Justin got right up against Mack and grabbed the shower head with one hand and hooked his other arm around Mack. He thrust in hard, fast jabs, needing release, needing to be inside Mack forever but also needing to feel Mack take him all over again.

He was winded from the athletic movements of his hips smacking faster and faster against Mack, from the grip he held on the shower head and on Mack. Justin hitched one leg up and got his toes on the rim of the tub. He didn't have much room because of the wall, but the angle allowed him to thrust in deeper.

"Come on, give it to me," Mack snarled, and damned if it didn't send Justin into orbit. He fucked into Mack mindlessly as his cock spurted his load.

"I'm not gonna be able to stand for you to fuck me," he said a few minutes later.

Mack's grin was devilish and had Justin's dick twitching. "Who said I wanted you to?"

And in short order, Justin was out of the shower, his knees on the several towels Mack had thrown on the floor. Justin was ass up with his arms hooked over the side of the tub.

"Yeah, this is how I want you," Mack said from behind him. "I have this gorgeous view. Your balls are hanging down, your dick, too. I can see your hole when you—" Mack popped him on the ass and Justin squeaked in surprise. "Unclench your ass, bub. Show me where you want me."

Justin spread his knees a little more and tipped his butt up. He didn't have any shame. Wouldn't have any, if it'd get Mack in him faster. "Come on, Mack. Put that big cock of yours where it belongs."

Mack knelt behind him. He ran his hands down Justin's buttocks and back up them, scratching them lightly. "Where does it belong, Jus?"

"Whatever hole of mine you want it in," he answered, slightly exasperated, because it seemed like an obvious answer to him.

Mack pulled him up by the shoulder. He got between Justin and the tub and sat on the rim. "Suck me, then. Suck me until I'm dripping wet, then I'm gonna fuck you."

Shit, he'd created a sensual monster. Mack was going to kill him, talking like that. Doing it, too, Justin thought as he bent to lap at Mack's cock.

"Open up," Mack said, holding his shaft still and straight, aiming it at Justin's lips. "Let me in."

Justin opened his mouth, and Mack pushed right in. He cupped Justin's nape and Justin bobbed down as Mack thrust.

"Oh, yeah. Damn, maybe I'll just fuck your mouth instead. Feels so good." Mack held Justin in place and proceeded to do just that for a few minutes. Justin found a thrill in the way Mack held him still and took over. He was looking forward to sucking the cum right out of Mack, was counting on it when Mack pulled out and ran a thumb over his lips.

"You look good like this, Jus, down on your knees, your lips all swollen, dazed and maybe a little disappointed I didn't come in your mouth." Mack leaned in and kissed him, sucking on his bottom lip.

Justin didn't care what he heard, he didn't whimper. He must have had water in his ears still.

"But I want to feel you like this," Mack said, standing up. He moved around to Justin's back. "Get back over the tub, and brace yourself. I'm not going to be able to be gentle."

"I don't need gentle. I'm not a virgin," Justin told him.

"Not far from it, though," Mack pointed out. He pushed a digit into Justin's hole before he could argue about it anymore. "So tight."

There was the sound of that same conditioner bottle being opened, then a wet glob of it hit Justin right at the top of his crack. He was going to need another shower when they finished.

Mack smeared the stuff down and at least two fingers speared into him. Justin arched into the burn, his balls throbbing with the need to come again.

"I hope that's good enough." Mack did something, turned his fingers around in him or spread them, maybe even added more of them, because Justin's ring suddenly felt stretched incredibly wide. "Damn, that's pretty. Beautiful, even."

Then Mack's fingers were gone and Justin was empty. He didn't stay that way for long. Mack had his cock right there, pushing it into Justin, filling him up with that perfect shaft.

"Damn, I can't—" Mack groaned and he hooked his arms around Justin, one hand unerringly finding Justin's length. "Oh, yeah," Mack said right before he thrust in fully.

Justin slapped a hand against the other side of the tub. Mack withdrew almost fully before pushing back in. He stroked Justin's cock in counter-rhythm to his thrusts, and Justin's poor mind couldn't keep up with which was the more pleasurable sensation. He didn't even try after the first thirty seconds.

Mack grunted and cursed and told him how perfect he was, how he loved every one of Justin's freckles, how much he reminded Mack of that ornery red stallion. Justin soaked it all in, letting Mack's words fill him with a hope and love that was greater than anything he'd ever known.

When Mack kissed him on his nape, then his neck, and sucked up a mark, Justin lost it, coming as he humped Mack's hand. Mack ploughed into him for another half dozen thrusts, then he was warming Justin's inner walls with his spunk.

It was one of those perfect moments that he'd remember in detail until the day he died. Justin smiled and held it in his heart.

* * * *

Justin and Mack had managed to shower again, because Mack had kind of made a mess of Justin between the cum and the conditioner. Afterwards, Justin had bandaged Mack's hand again. The wound wasn't bad, Justin assured him, but Mack didn't want to risk seeing anything gross. His hand sure hadn't bothered him when he'd been fucking Justin, but then Mack figured he could probably be bleeding to death from a dozen different wounds and still fuck Justin without being aware of his own injuries.

They lay down on the bed and dozed off after Justin called and asked Craig to come make sure Leo was gone. Mack wasn't sure how he felt about Craig still. The guy was just too lethal or something. Maybe with time he'd be more comfortable around him.

Mack rolled to his side, content to watch Justin sleep. He had his mouth slightly open and soft puffs of air slipped out of that pretty mouth. Justin's lips were still swollen, and a deep pink from sucking Mack's dick earlier. It was a fantastic look on the tough Marine. Mack took a visual stroll down Justin's body, admiring the thick thighs coated with red-gold hair, the swell of that rounded butt and even the curve of Justin's arches.

Maybe he had a budding foot fetish. His pecker was sure trying to rise again while he studied the way Justin's feet were made, the ankles sturdy and his toes stubby and sprinkled with hair.

Mack raked his gaze back up before he did something freaky, like hump Justin's foot. He almost jumped when he found Justin watching him. There was a slow roil of desire in his gut, and Mack wondered if they would ever get enough of each other. He didn't think so.

Justin reached for him, touching Mack's cheek. He spoke so softly, Mack had to strain to hear him. "God, Mack. Do you have any idea how much I've missed you? I felt like I was missing all of my heart for so long."

Mack imagined they'd be trading sweet words for a long time to come after what they'd been through. "I know. I missed you too, more than I know how to tell you in words." He settled back down beside Justin, the better to pull him close and kiss him. He'd have sworn Justin's lips tasted sweeter now that they were ripe and berry-pink for him.

"I love you like crazy." Mack kissed Justin again, moaning, needing.

Justin nipped his lips, his tongue, and his hands were on Mack's nipples in an instant, pinching, twisting. Mack decided he was becoming some kind of nipple-pain-whore, because he really liked what was going on there.

Justin rolled them over, coming down on top of Mack. He wasn't teasing Mack's tits any more, instead propping himself up on his elbows so he could stare down at Mack. "You know I came back as soon as I could, when my last tour ended and I got out. I didn't even wait a day, just packed my shit and drove."

"No, I didn't know that. You hadn't said. Where were you stationed last?" Mack asked.

Justin grinned. "My last tour was actually in Hawaii, but I ended up in Tucson for a month or so before I was out. Hawaii wasn't bad. I'd love to take you there sometime."

Mack tried to picture it, but his mind blanked out every image he'd ever seen of Hawaii. "You know I've never even left the state of Texas before, right?"

"Never?" Justin asked, sounding sceptical. "You never even headed to Mexico?"

"Why?" Mack shrugged. "I think I've just kind of been waiting for you like I told Leo. I might not have known it here, in my head, but in my heart, I never could believe you'd stay away forever."

"I swear I was just waiting for the old man to pass on. Once he died, I knew you were out of his crosshairs."

"I wondered why you didn't come back for his funeral, but I thought you were probably overseas somewhere." Mack frowned. "Your father would brag about you."

Justin frowned, too. "Yeah, he would have. I didn't keep him updated on anything I did. As far as I was concerned, he was dead to me the minute he threatened your life. He had his ways of finding out what was happening with me. Every now and then he'd send me a postcard reminding me he was still here, still watching. I'll probably go to hell for hating the man so much."

Mack shook his head. "I don't think so. I don't think some people are ever meant to be parents, and I don't know what goes wrong, how or who decides they should have kids, but someone, somewhere, screws up. My dad could be violent, but he usually stopped short of hurting me too bad. I think he blamed me for my mother dying, but it wasn't like I could help it. She had an aneurysm when I was about two."

"I remember hearing about that, maybe when our dads were talking or something. I don't even know what happened to my mother. I was told she ran off, but knowing my father's temper…" Justin sucked his bottom lip in between his teeth then released it. "She could be buried anywhere in this state. I'd be more inclined to believe that. I've never been able to track down anything about her."

"You tried?" Mack asked.

"Yeah. Thought maybe she'd run off from her husband, not her kid. He'd never have let her have me, even if he didn't want me." Justin huffed and rested some of his weight on Mack. "Enough of that. I don't have an answer, and I doubt I ever will. I'm here now, and you're not getting rid of me ever."

"Sounds good to me. But tell me, did you have to buy a ranch?"

Justin chuckled and shifted onto one arm. He used his other hand to caress Mack's side and feather his fingers over Mack's hip. "I figured it would be best to have some leverage if necessary. Then once you agreed to work the JMR's horses—" Justin sat up as suddenly as if he'd been poked in the flank. "Hey, did I tell you what that stands for?"

Mack was confused for a second then he shook his head. "Nope, you haven't."

"Justin Mack Ranch," Justin said, looking so pleased with himself that Mack was tempted to poke him in the ribs. Instead he sat up as well and got his hands on Justin's gloriously sweet ass.

"Justin Mack Ranch," Mack murmured. "Huh. If my brain hadn't been short on blood lately, I might have caught on to that one sooner." He took Justin down again, this time coming out on top. His cock aligned very nicely with Justin's and Mack wasn't the only one who moaned.

"So tell me, bub, what are we going to do with two ranches?"

Justin looked adorably confused, like he hadn't planned that far ahead. "How the hell should I know?" he said, confirming Mack's suspicions. "I didn't get much further with my plan than where it's at now. Craig's been running everything except what I have to handle since I'm the owner. You're the cowboy. What do you think we ought to do with them?"

Mack grinned. "Well, hell on hoofs, Justin, there aren't many people who can say someone loved them enough to buy a ranch they didn't have a clue how to run just so they could be close to them." Actually, that was kind of a confusing mouthful. "We'll have to make sure our kids get it right."

"Kids?" Justin fairly squeaked. "Like, the little two-legged critters that cry and snot and poop all the time, or the cute four-legged kind?"

Mack swatted Justin's hip. "The kind we're gonna have, whether we adopt or find surrogates, I don't much care how we do it. I just want a family with you."

"But our parents—" Justin began.

"We aren't them," Mack informed him. "We aren't. We'll be good to our kids, and they won't know what it means to be abused or threatened with their lives. They won't know anything but the unconditional love their daddies have for them until they're old enough to see outside of that. We'll raise them, and love them, and use the parenting we know is bad to ensure we do it the good way. Like a parenting what-not-to-do, courtesy of our upbringings. We just mostly do the opposite of that."

Justin stared up at him with something like hope and fear tangled up in his expression. "You really want kids?"

Mack nodded. "Always have. I figure six or so, girls and boys. Close together in age, if we can manage it."

"This is important to you?"

"It's not a deal-breaker if you don't want any," Mack admitted reluctantly, "but yeah, having kids would mean a lot to me. I don't need an answer now, but I'd like you to think about it. Maybe in a year or two you'll be ready. We don't want to wait too long. I don't want to be sixty when our first one is graduating high school."

"And college—if we have any kids, I mean," Justin amended.

"And college." Mack grinned at Justin. "So I think we should combine the ranches, because we're maybe gonna have a herd of kids to parse it out to when we get ancient. I think that settles everything, at least for now. Don't you?"

Mack rubbed his cock against Justin's, getting a moan from the sexy red devil. "Sounds like a 'yes, Mack' to me."

Mack slid down Justin's body, stopping only once he was head and shoulders between Justin's thighs. Mack brought his hand down and brushed the dark red patch of hair at the base of that mouth-watering cock. He bent down, gently sucking the cap into his mouth. Mack ran his tongue over the slit then down under the rim to tease Justin's frenulum.

He brought two fingers to his mouth, licking them in between licking and sucking on Justin's shaft. When he had those digits slick enough, he trailed them down Justin's balls, then farther back until he found that tight, hot muscle hidden there.

Justin's pucker was still warm and puffy from their earlier fucking. Mack imagined his hole was in the same shape. "Too sore?" he asked as he teased that ruched skin.

"Nuh-uh," Justin scraped out.

Mack swallowed Justin's cock down as far as he could take then, while at the same time pushing his fingers into Justin's ass.

"Mack!" Justin writhed, trying to get more fingers, more mouth, Mack wasn't sure which. Maybe, like Mack had done earlier, Justin was trying to get more of both.

"Don't stop, Mack, please, baby, let me shoot down your throat," Justin pleaded.

Mack could feel the way Justin's inner walls kept contracting around his fingers. He knew Justin's balls were drawn up, that sac wrinkled and close to his body. Justin's cock swelled against his tongue, one thick vein in particular seeming to pulse.

He sucked hard and pushed a third finger into Justin's hole. Cum squirted from Justin's dick as Justin moaned. Mack sucked and licked Justin's shaft, holding his fingers still where he was touching Justin's gland. Once he'd wrung every last drop out of Justin, he eased his fingers free and let Justin's cock slip from his mouth.

Feeling his lover come apart had almost made Mack come too. He'd held off, though, because he had other plans for his dick. He levered himself back down beside Justin. Justin slanted him a look.

"Huh, what do you know," Mack mused. "I have got to do better next time. You should have been too wrung out to even open your eyes."

Justin's attempt to look disgruntled was cute. Mack laughed and kissed his brow.

"That look ain't gonna work, bub, not after you just told me very loudly, as a matter of fact, how thoroughly you enjoyed my mouth and fingers." He brushed his lips over Justin's, intending to keep it soft and sweet. Mack let out a squeak of surprise—like he had a damned squeaky girl living inside him or something—when Justin pinched his ass.

"Now," Justin purred, "I do remember hearing something along the lines of turnabout and fair play, cowboy. I wouldn't want you feeling neglected or anything like that."

Mack's cock jerked, leaking a warm drop of pre-cum onto the sheets. "What, exactly, do you have in mind?"

Grinning, Justin got off the bed and picked something up from the floor. Mack's dick leaked like a faucet when he saw Justin holding the Stetson.

"I told you one day you were gonna ride me wearing nothing but this hat and a smile. Today seems like a good day to make good on my word, don't you think?"

Mack's cock and his mind were on the same boat. "I do have some vague memory of hearing that, and it is really important to keep your promises. Got to be dependable." Mack smiled as Justin leapt onto the bed. Oh yeah, he sure loved his man, and that was his last coherent thought for a good, long while.

Epilogue

Mack and Justin stood at the corral, watching the red stallion paw the ground. That horse was still every bit as obnoxious as the day it had arrived on Mack's ranch. Of course, he hadn't even worked with the evil thing. Justin had been keeping him busy, and frankly many days his ass was too well-used to take a pounding from a horse set on killing him.

"It's your turn to try and give him some sugar cubes," Mack said, keeping a straight face as Justin glared at him.

"Fuck no. That mean son of a bitch tried to rip off my fingers last time I stuck them over the rail. He doesn't deserve a treat." Justin scowled. "'Hold your hand out flat,' Mack said. 'Keep it steady no matter what. Horses don't bite unless you curl your hand up and they think your fingers are snacks'." Justin pointed at him. "Sound familiar? You almost had me missing some fingers, and your ass would not be happy if that happened."

Mack couldn't very well dispute any of that. "He never tried to bite my fingers. Maybe he's just jealous, and remember — it's not a reward, it's a bribe. There's a difference. He doesn't get them if he acts like a dick." Mack took some cubes from his shirt pocket and held them out to Justin. "Come on, don't be a baby. I promise if he bites anything off, we can have it reattached as long as he don't swallow it."

Justin snorted, reminding Mack a lot of a certain cantankerous red stallion. "I refuse to be goaded into risking my fingers, cowboy. Not gonna happen, but I've been thinking…" He glanced back at the stallion then turned sideways, facing Mack but still keeping the horse in his peripheral sight. "Maybe we should just let him be, so to speak. Use him for stud if we can. I kind of like the evil bastard like this, all angry and righteous and untamed. He's beautiful, like raw power set free on this earth, and I know it sounds silly probably, but I just would hate to see his spirit lessened from this brilliant, fiery sun to a dim glow."

Justin tipped his chin towards the horse, which looked to be readying for another charge at them. Mack placed his hand on his lover's arm, urging him to step back a little farther away from the fence. Diablo — that was the only name that fit the red horse — had taken to trying to knock them on their ass by swatting at them with his big, hard head.

Mack thought about what Justin had said as he watched Diablo run full force at them, and Mack went from backing them up slowly to hauling ass backwards. Justin was right beside him, stumbling and cursing.

"On second thought, let's geld him," Justin huffed. "Maybe if he loses his nuts he won't be so fucking angry. You'd think it'd be the other way around. If someone cut my balls off, I'd be out for revenge."

"So imagine this." Mack waved at Diablo, who looked damned pleased with himself. If a horse could smirk, that was exactly what Diablo was doing. "Our luck he'd react like you. Then we'd all be killed by a more psychotic, rampaging beast." He didn't think Diablo was that bad. They could tame him, Mack knew they could, but he agreed with Justin. There was something majestic and wild and beautiful they'd lose if they did. "I think your idea to leave him alone is a great idea. You don't really want to mess with breaking him. Neither do I."

"I'm not as sure as you are that we could break that devil," Justin muttered. "And you sure gave in easy on that."

Mack grinned and cupped his balls. "Jesus, Justin, I'm not in a hurry to have these busted by Diablo. I kind of like having them, and he'd likely buck 'em right up into my belly. Do you want to get on that animal?" He knew the answer to that, and didn't even give Justin the chance to say it.

"Besides," Mack whispered against Justin's lips. "I have my very own red-haired devil to ride, and he's much, much more fun to mount, you know?" And damned if Justin didn't drag him inside and have Mack do just that.

About the Author

A native Texan, Bailey spends her days spinning stories around in her head, which has contributed to more than one incident of tripping over her own feet. Evenings are reserved for pounding away at the keyboard, as are early morning hours. Sleep? Doesn't happen much. Writing is too much fun, and there are too many characters bouncing about, tapping on Bailey's brain demanding to be let out.

Caffeine and chocolate are permanent fixtures in Bailey's office and are never far from hand at any given time. Removing either of those necessities from Bailey's presence can result in what is know as A Very, Very Scary Bailey and is not advised under any circumstances.

Bailey Bradford loves to hear from readers. You can find her contact information, website details and author profile page at http://www.total-e-bound.com.

Total-E-Bound Publishing

www.total-e-bound.com

Take a look at our exciting range of literagasmic™
erotic romance titles and discover pure quality
at Total-E-Bound.